WINTER DREAMS

I started to wander down the aisles of the general store, when suddenly a door in the back opened and I turned to see him. As he walked toward me I inspected the strong, angled lines of his face, and the dark, nearly black hair that he pushed out of his eyes with one hand as he rested a box on the floor.

Mrs. Cartwright walked up to the boy. "This is my son, Michael."

She gestured with her hand, then touched the boy's shirt sleeve. He turned and smiled at Helen, but ignored me.

It figures, I thought. This Michael Cartwright was acting just like a lot of good-looking guys I knew—completely stuck-up.

"Happy to meet you," he said to Helen, still ignoring me. Then, picking up the empty carton, he went out the same way he had come in without glancing back.

What a waste, I thought. *The one person in this wilderness who looks slightly interesting, and he doesn't even notice me.*

Bantam Sweet Dreams Romances
Ask your bookseller for the books you have missed

Winter Dreams

Barbara Conklin

BANTAM BOOKS
TORONTO · NEW YORK · LONDON · SYDNEY · AUCKLAND

RL 6, IL age 11 and up

WINTER DREAMS
A Bantam Book / March 1988

Cover photo by Pat Hill.

ISBN 0-553-27062-1

Published simultaneously in the United States and Canada

Bantam Books are published by Bantam Books, a division of Bantam Doubleday Dell Publishing Group, Inc. Its trademark, consisting of the words "Bantam Books" and the portrayal of a rooster, is Registered in U.S. Patent and Trademark Office and in other countries. Marca Registrada. Bantam Books, 666 Fifth Avenue, New York, New York 10103.

PRINTED IN THE UNITED STATES OF AMERICA

O   0 9 8 7 6 5 4 3 2 1

To Librarians: they sort, stamp, catalog, repair, preserve, and watch over our most treasured possessions. May joy and happiness be their companions as they labor on with their most honored tasks.

Chapter One

"I can't believe we actually own it!" my step-mother, Helen, cried as my dad pulled the car into the driveway of our new house.

"I can't believe it, either," I muttered unhappily to myself.

"Now, Anna," chided my grandmother, who was sitting next to me. "Don't sound so low. You'll feel better in a few minutes."

Grandma was convinced I was suffering from car sickness, which wouldn't have been surprising, considering that we'd just spent an hour and a half on the narrow, twisting road to Blue Mountain. But the sick, hollow feeling in the pit of my stomach had nothing to do with the ride. It came from the awful realization that the three-story house in front of me, so far from everything I'd ever known, was the place I was going to have to call home from then on.

My father winked at Helen as he took the keys from the ignition. "Now the real fun begins," he announced.

"You call unpacking fun?" my grandmother asked. Like the rest of us, she'd spent the past two weeks sorting through a lifetime of belongings, deciding which to get rid of and which to pack. It'd been terribly hard for me to part with my old things, especially my ratty old stuffed animals. So it must have been agonizing for her to throw away things she had held on to for all the years she had lived with us.

"I'm not talking about unpacking, Mom," my father said. "I mean fixing this place up, getting ready for the opening."

Oh, yes, the grand opening. You see, this wasn't just an ordinary house. To the rest of the world it would soon be known as the Willows Inn, a bed-and-breakfast hotel. Around our family it was simply known as "Helen's dream."

For as long as I'd known her, which was since I was seven and Dad first brought her home, Helen had run a beauty shop in Rutherford, the town in southern California where I'd lived my whole life. But what she really wanted to do was own one of those cozy little places where people could go to spend a weekend away from the

2

pressures of the city. I can't think of a Saturday when she didn't drag my father from one real estate agent to another searching for the perfect house. Long ago she had decided that the mountains would be the ideal location, but they never really had the money to buy until a few months ago, when Helen's mother died. She had left enough of an inheritance to finally make Helen's dream come true.

So there we were, a month into what was supposed to be the best summer of my life, suddenly transported into a new way of living. No one seemed to care that Helen's dream meant that I'd be taken away from everything I'd ever known—my home, all my friends, my favorite places, and even my very first summer job.

Truthfully, it wasn't much of a job. I'd only been working part-time as an assistant counselor at a children's day camp in Rutherford, but I'd always liked kids and liked thinking up games and activities for them. I'd also gotten to work with Tommy Preston, a real cute guy from Caldwell. I sort of liked him, and he had just started to pay attention to me. But now I'd never know if anything could have happened between us—and I blamed Helen for it.

Helen didn't seem to notice. Neither did my dad. He'd always been a life insurance claims manager, and over the years Helen's dream had

3

become his dream, too. When she found this house he didn't think twice about quitting his job, and ever since then all he could talk about was how he was going to spend his days designing and refinishing furniture for the inn. Even Grandma got caught up in the spirit of a new adventure—once she was told she could cook and bake for all the guests at the inn.

So I had no one to turn to. My friends in Rutherford understood, but there wasn't much they could do about it. My best friend, Susan Keller, even threw me a going-away party. But that only made me feel worse. I hated goodbyes more than anything, and seeing all my friends smiling and having a good time only made me realize how much I was going to miss Rutherford.

The ride to the new house intensified that feeling. The road swung through the town of Blue Mountain, which consisted of nothing more than a general store, a gas station, a restaurant, a place to rent canoes and camping stuff, and a couple of bars. That was it. No malls, no McDonald's, and no people.

Just then Helen tugged on my bare arm, jolting me back to reality. "Come on out, Anna. I can't wait to show you your new room. You're going to love it!"

That was just like Helen, bubbly and optimistic about everything. I managed a smile and swung my long legs out of the car. In junior high some of the boys used to call me Anna Willow Tree because my last name is Willows and I used to tower over everyone. But by the time I'd entered high school the boys had caught up, and I realized that being tall wasn't such a bad thing after all.

The cool mountain air made me feel a little better. "So this is it," I said, gazing up at the stately Victorian house. It was perched on a hill, and from my vantage point in the driveway, I could look down at the sweeping view of the valley below us. Rolling hills covered with pines, sagebrush, and sequoias were spread in front of me like a patchwork quilt. The house was beautiful, but I wasn't about to admit it to Helen.

She grabbed my hand. "Let's go inside. There's so much to see."

"What about the boxes?" I pointed to the crammed station wagon.

"I'll take care of those," Dad said, smiling. "Go check out your room."

I didn't see what the big deal was. Nothing could ever replace my room back home. The wall behind my bed was still covered with the flower print wallpaper my real mother had picked out not too long before she had died. And even though the room wasn't very big, I had made it my own, hanging movie-star posters and fashion layouts from magazines on the other walls. I was pretty sure that I wanted to be a fashion designer someday.

Helen guided me past the stained-glass front entryway, through a walnut-paneled hall and a gigantic kitchen to a winding staircase at the back of that room. "Your bedroom's on the third floor," she said. "We thought you'd like this one because there's enough room for you to entertain your friends."

My heart fell again when she mentioned friends. In a town as tiny as Blue Mountain there wouldn't be too many friends.

We made our way up the narrow wooden staircase. "As you know," Helen said, "we bought the place furnished. I think you're going to like what's here, but if you don't, we can talk about redecorating—"

Just then we reached the top of the stairs, and through the open door I got my first glimpse of my new room. I didn't want to admit it, but it was beautiful. There was a canopied four-poster bed and an easy chair covered and trimmed with blue-and-white fabric and ruffles. The draperies on the two oval-shaped windows were made of the same material. Covering the dark, shiny wood floor was a large braided rug. It all looked as if it'd been transported out of a decorator's showroom. Only the movers' boxes, stacked neatly inside the huge walk-in closet, suggested that the room was intended for a real person.

My eyes must have given me away. "Just wait till you see the rest," Helen said excitedly. She opened a white door at the far end of the room. "And right through here is your private bathroom."

It wasn't just a bathroom. A thick, yellow fluffy rug sat on top of an endless black- and white-tiled floor. In one corner was a funny-looking old bathtub with big claw feet, in another a white-enameled closet with more than enough shelves to fit my blow dryer and makeup. There were even hand-painted flowers on the small black tiles that lined the door and window.

I walked back into the bedroom and sat on the white candlewick bedspread. "All this space for me?" I said, still not quite believing it.

"Isn't it great?" Helen sat down beside me and gave me a hug. "I'm so glad you like it," she said. "It means a lot to me, you know."

I stiffened under her caress. Of course I knew the inn meant a lot to her. But even though the room was beautiful, there was still a hollow feeling inside me. The room looked too perfect, too unreal. I didn't feel as if they'd ever belong to me. "I'd better help Dad unpack," I said, rising.

Helen stood up, too, looking slightly hurt. "You're right," she said softly. "We've got so much to do."

We found Dad and Grandma in what would soon be the dining room unpacking boxes that the movers had delivered the day before. Dad looked up when he heard us come in. "So what do you think, kitten?"

That twinkle was still in his eyes, and I couldn't bear to tell him how much I wanted to go home. "It's nice, Dad," I managed to say.

He was too busy searching through the boxes to notice the forced cheerfulness in my voice. "Helen," he said, "have you seen my tape measure? I thought it was in my tool box."

"It was," Helen answered. "But then I took it out the last time we were here to check the length of the kitchen shelves, and I put it in—" She looked at the stack of boxes with dismay. "I don't know which box I put it in," she said wearily. "And it will take us days to get through all of these. Maybe we'd better buy a new one. I'll go to that store we passed on the way in."

"Good idea," he said, his head still buried in a carton. "Take Anna with you. Show her around."

Two minutes later Helen and I were back in the station wagon. This time I got to ride in front, but that queasy feeling remained.

Helen didn't mention my room again. Instead, she talked about Blue Mountain, telling me what I had pretty much figured out for myself—that it was a small town, depending almost entirely on tourists for its income. "Pray for snow," she said as we drove past the road to a nearby ski slope. "We expect the winter to be our busiest time."

I nodded absently as she continued talking. "Your dad and I are going to be very busy these next few weeks getting the inn ready to open. I'm afraid we're not going to be able to spend very much time with you, Anna. I hope you understand."

"Sure," I said. "It's no problem."

"It won't be so bad," she went on. "You've got four weeks till school starts, plenty of time to make friends."

"What friends?" I said. "There can't be more than two people in this entire town."

"Oh, come now, Anna. There are plenty of people on the mountain. Things are just more spread out here, that's all."

"And where am I supposed to meet them?" I asked. "It's not that easy. Did you ever have to make new friends? Did you ever have to switch high schools at the beginning of *your* junior year?"

Helen frowned slightly. "I know the move is

hard on you, Anna. Starting out in a new place is never easy. But you've never had trouble talking to people. I'm sure you'll make plenty of new friends soon."

"I guess," I said, but as we pulled into the small parking lot beside the general store I saw little reason to be hopeful. There were a couple of small kids on bikes, some older people dressed for hiking, and several camper trucks parked in the lot. But even though it was the middle of a gorgeous, sunny summer afternoon, there was no one my age in sight.

Inside the store a plump woman about Helen's age was standing behind the counter. "Good afternoon," she said. "Can I help you?"

"I'm looking for a tape measure," Helen answered. "My name's Helen Willows. And this is my daughter, Anna. We just bought the old Turner place."

There she goes again, I thought, *telling a stranger her life story*. That was the thing about Helen. She loved to talk. Also, she always introduced me as her daughter, but right then I wasn't in the mood to correct her.

The woman behind the counter actually seemed interested in what Helen was saying. "Welcome to Blue Mountain," she said. "I'm Emma Cartwright, and I'm glad to hear you're neighbors.

So it's a tape measure you need, huh? I'll be back in a second."

I couldn't imagine how the woman would find one. The place was a hodgepodge of everything from canned goods, magazines, ice cream, and milk to newspapers, books, hardware and fishing supplies, and even clothes.

Sure enough, a moment later Mrs. Cartwright returned from one of the aisles with a tape measure and a jar of jam. "The jam is on the house," she said as she handed it to Helen. "I make it myself. It's my way of welcoming you to Blue Mountain."

"How nice of you!" Helen was acting as though she'd just won the lottery. "We'll really use this. We're turning the place into a bed-and-breakfast inn."

Mrs. Cartwright rested her hands on the weathered wooden counter. "That's wonderful! We need a place like that around here. It'll bring us more business, too, I imagine. What are you going to call it?"

"Willows Inn," Helen said, "since our name is Willows and there are two beautiful willow trees in the front yard."

"Oh, yes, I remember," Mrs. Cartwright said. "Why, those trees—"

I really wasn't interested in their conversation, so I started to wander down the aisles, looking at all the things on the shelves.

It was then that a door in the back of the store opened, and I turned to see him. I don't really know what surprised me more—the boy's dramatic good looks or the simple fact that he was my age. Actually he looked a little older, about seventeen or eighteen, but that was close enough. As he walked toward me I inspected the strong, angled lines of his face, and the dark, nearly black hair that he pushed out of his eyes with one hand as he rested a box on the floor.

Pulling a knife out of his back pocket, he slit open the box and began to stock cans of tomato paste on an empty shelf. He lined them up meticulously, never once looking at me or my stepmother.

Finally Helen paid for the tape measure, and Mrs. Cartwright walked up to the boy. "Mrs. Willows, Anna, this is my son, Michael." She gestured with her hand, then touched the boy's shirt sleeve. He turned and smiled at Helen, but ignored me.

It figures, I thought. This Michael Cartwright was acting just like a lot of good-looking guys I knew—completely stuck-up. That's the way it was with guys like that. Knowing they're good-

looking does something to wreck their person-
alities.

"Happy to meet you," he said to Helen, still
ignoring me. Then, picking up the empty carton, he went out the same way he had come in
without glancing back.

What a waste, I thought. *The one person in
this wilderness who looks slightly interesting,
and he doesn't even notice me.* Still, even though
I'd just about written off this guy as a hopeless
snob, I couldn't help thinking about how gorgeous he was.

That thought only made the ride home more
unbearable than the ride to the store. Here I'd
finally met someone my age—and he wouldn't
give me the time of day.

Chapter Two

I awoke the following morning as I usually did, to the sound of my canary, Yellow Bird. For a brief moment I pretended I was back in my old bed in Rutherford, but the bright sun spilling into the room ruined that fantasy in an instant. No, I realized, the day before hadn't been a nightmare. It was all too depressingly real.

Quickly, I pulled on a pair of shorts and a T-shirt and padded down the stairs to the kitchen. I may have felt awful about the move, but it didn't stop me from being hungry. Besides, Grandma's hearty breakfasts almost always made me feel better.

Just as I expected, Grandma was already standing in front of the stove, whipping up a batch of pancakes. She loved to sing, and that day she was humming a tune from *The Sound of Music.* "It's a beautiful day, isn't it, Anna?" She sounded as chipper as Yellow Bird. Whatever regrets she might have had about moving seemed to have vanished.

It must have been the kitchen that did it. It was a dream room, everything my grandmother could ever want: a walk-in pantry, oversize sinks, double-door refrigerator, and three long butcher-block counters. I saw a carton of eggs next to a mixing bowl on the other side of the room. Grandma was probably already planning on baking after breakfast.

I went to the refrigerator for a glass of milk, but to my surprise there wasn't any. "Where's the milk?" I asked.

"I used the last of it to make pancakes," she answered.

Great, I thought as I took the hot pancakes to the table. What good were pancakes without milk? Obviously, my first day on Blue Mountain was getting off to a rotten start. "Where are Dad and Helen?"

"Your father's down in the basement setting up his workshop. Helen's working on the living room." She looked at me thoughtfully. "You know, we're also out of coffee, baking soda, and about five other things. How about if I make a list and you go to the store after breakfast? It would give you something to do."

I nodded dutifully, not really wanting to go but not wanting to refuse my grandmother, either. I took my time eating, trying to put off the rest of the day. But I couldn't help noticing how happy Grandma looked as she unpacked her favorite china. "I always wanted a kitchen like this, Anna," she told me.

"What was wrong with the kitchen in the old house?" I asked. I could hear the little-girl pout in my voice, but I didn't try to control it.

She smiled. "Anna, I know you miss the old place, but you'll like it here, too. Just give it some time."

She sounded just like Helen. It was exactly what I didn't need to hear, I thought glumly. Quickly I finished the rest of my breakfast. "I'd better be going," I said as I excused myself from the table.

I found my bike beside the garage, got my grandma's list and some money from Dad, and pedaled down the road toward the general store.

About halfway there I realized I hadn't even brushed my hair or put on mascara. The thought made me laugh. Who would I be looking good for? Certainly not Michael Cartwright, who hadn't noticed me yesterday when I looked halfway decent. And I doubted I'd run into anyone else my age.

My bike wobbled as I turned into the parking

lot of the store. The gravel made it almost impossible to steer. I turned the front wheel slightly to the right, attempting to edge closer to the store, toward the front steps. My eyes were focused on those steps, which is why I didn't notice that something was coming at me from the left.

Before I knew it, I was colliding. I could feel myself fall off the bike, knowing in that split second I was going to crash to the ground, yet helpless to do anything about it. Sure enough I landed on my right knee first, my bike coming to a rest with a thud on top of my ankle. Gravel dug into my knee, and blood began to trickle down my leg. There were a few scrapes on my palms, too, but otherwise I was still in one piece.

"Hey, watch it!" said an angry voice.

For the first time I looked at the person who'd run into me. Michael Cartwright was kneeling on the other side of the bike. Not only was he a snob, he had the nerve to blame me for an accident he caused!

"Why don't *you* watch it?" I shouted back.

I looked down at my shorts. They had been white before the accident but were now gray with dust and grease stains across the front. "Look what you've done!"

Quickly he stood up and brushed some gravel

from his jeans, apparently none the worse from the encounter. He looked a little contrite as he ran his fingers through his hair. "I'm sorry, I didn't hear you coming," he said stiffly.

"That's no excuse," I snapped.

"Look, I said I'm sorry," he repeated, more forcefully this time.

Finally he was looking at me, but I sensed something different about him. His stare was off to the right a little, and when he tilted his head slightly I suddenly realized the truth. "Oh, my gosh, you're blind," I blurted out.

"Everyone around here knows that. Who are you?" he asked.

"Anna. Anna Willows. I came by yesterday with my stepmother. We just moved here. From Rutherford. That's down in the valley." The words just poured out. I was rambling on exactly like Helen. I felt so awkward, so embarrassed—and so sad for Michael. I had just torn into him for scraping my knee, and he had real problems to deal with. I was glad he couldn't see what must have been the look of horror on my face.

"Look, I hope you're not hurt," he said. "Usually I can hear people coming." This time he sounded so concerned, so unlike the stuck-up guy I'd made him out to be.

"I'm sorry," I said. "I should have been more careful."

He laughed gruffly. "Sometimes I think I should wear a sign that says, 'Watch out. Blind guy approaching.' You're not the first person I've met this way."

I didn't know what to say. I'd never met anyone who was blind, and I was filled with questions, like how long he'd been blind and what it was like and whether he used a Seeing Eye dog. But I couldn't come right out and ask them. I'd already been rude enough. "Uh, I'd better be going," I said.

"Didn't you want something from the store?"

"Oh, yeah," I said awkwardly. "Milk and coffee and some other stuff."

As I walked up the steps Mrs. Cartwright was coming to the screen door. "Michael, are you all right?" she called. Then she noticed me and my bloody leg. "For heaven's sake, you're hurt! What happened?"

"Just another friendly encounter," Michael said as he joined us on the steps. The sarcasm in his voice was unmistakable. I wanted to pretend the whole thing had never happened.

"Michael, go inside and mind the counter while I tend to Anna."

Before I had a chance to protest, Mrs. Cartwright led me to the back of the store where she sat me in an old rocking chair. "Did you need another tape measure?" she asked, smiling as she examined my knee.

"No, groceries this time." I winced as she began to clean the cuts with alcohol. "My grandmother gave me a whole list."

"Well, we'll see what we can do about that. Meanwhile"—she reached for a box of bandages—"you've scraped yourself up pretty good." From where we sat we could hear what sounded like a group of people entering the store. Immediately she stood up. "I'm sorry," she said, "but Michael's out there alone."

"That's okay," I said, taking the bandages from her. "I'll finish up."

She left the room, and I set to work, wondering if I'd ever outgrow scraped knees. I mean, it was pretty embarrassing to be sixteen years old and still have my knees look exactly as they did when I was in kindergarten—covered with bandages.

I put Mrs. Cartwright's first aid supplies back into the box she had stored them in, tested my knee gingerly, and went into the store.

The crowd must have left, because there was only one man standing at the counter. Mrs. Cartwright came up to me at once. "Are you all right?"

I assured her that I was.

"Well, then," she said briskly, "go ask Michael to fill your order."

Her tone of voice left no room for argument,

so somewhat hesitantly I turned to Michael. He had filled the order for another customer and was now coming toward me, returning a jar of preserves to the shelves. For a brief moment, I thought about my knee and how awful it looked, and then remembered that he couldn't see me. I wondered how he made his way around the store so effortlessly.

"You sure know your way around here," I said. I felt I had to say something before he collided with me again.

He stopped about a foot away from me. "I ought to. I've been here all my life."

"Just you and your mom?"

"Yeah." He nodded. "My dad died when I was a kid."

"Really? My mom died when I was six." It was a strange thing to have in common, the death of a parent, but that piece of information somehow made it easier for me to talk to him.

"Sorry to hear that," he said.

"I have a stepmother, Helen, the woman I was with yesterday. In fact it was her idea to move up here."

"You don't sound too thrilled with the idea," he said with a trace of a smile.

"Why should I be?"

"Don't you like the mountains?"

"What do you do around here?" I asked.

"Where I come from we've got malls, pools, restaurants, movies, the beach—lots of places to hang out. All I see around here are trees."

"You'll meet people," he said quickly as the bell over the door jangled. "If you'll excuse me, I've got some customers in front."

I looked beyond him at the middle-aged couple that had just entered the store, wondering if I'd get another chance to talk to him.

I realized I hadn't even asked him to fill my order, and it was a good half hour before I got the chance. There was suddenly a steady stream of customers, and Michael and Mrs. Cartwright had their hands full taking care of them. Even I got into the act, helping Mrs. Cartwright bag groceries.

In between I found myself thinking about and watching Michael. My interest wasn't just curiosity about a blind person. It was something more. He seemed at ease with the customers, chatting about last night's baseball scores and joking about someone in town. He knew most everyone by name, and I could tell that they all liked him. I watched Michael, thinking to myself, *If he weren't blind, I could be really attracted to him.* But then I realized with a jolt that he *was* blind and I was really attracted to him, anyway. There was something special about Michael Cartwright.

But not everything went smoothly for him. I saw him swear at himself when he gave a man a five-dollar bill instead of a one for change. The man gave back the five, but that didn't seem to make him feel better.

"You're lucky there are still some honest people around," I told him after the man had left and we were alone again.

"Sure," he grumbled, turning away. Then, slowly he turned back. "Anna? You're still here?"

"Yeah," I said, a little surprised myself. "I was supposed to ask you to fill my order, and then it got busy, and—"

"You're still waiting," he said, finishing for me. There was almost a smile on his face. "What do you need?"

I fished out Grandma's list, started to hand it to him, and then quickly drew it back. "You mean it isn't written in Braille?" he asked bitterly, somehow sensing what had happened.

"Don't worry, you're not missing anything," I said.

Immediately the mask went up again. "That's easy for you to say."

He had a point. I didn't know what it was like to be blind. "I'm sorry," I said.

"Not as sorry as I am," he replied.

"It must be rough," I said under my breath.

I hadn't expected him to hear me. "What?" he demanded.

"Oh—uh," I searched for words. "I, uh, was wondering how you made change. I mean, um, not being able to see and all." I could feel my face flush. Why was it that everything I said to him sounded so awful? Still, I was curious.

"By touch," he answered, the anger gone. "It's easy to tell the difference between coins. Paper money's tough. That's why my mom doesn't usually have me handle the register. But the woman who used to help us quit last week, and it's been a little hectic around here since."

"I've noticed. It seems like a lot for two people to handle."

"It's just as busy in the summer as it is during ski season," he explained. "Campers, hikers, people up for day trips. But I guess you know that."

"I'm just learning."

"Anna," Mrs. Cartwright called from the back, "did you get what you needed?"

"Almost," I called back, and read off the list to Michael, who collected all the items in about two minutes flat.

I realized with surprise that I didn't want to go. I liked talking to Michael. I felt that I was just getting to know him. I was paying for the food when I was struck by an inspiration. "Thanks for the first aid," I said to Mrs. Cartwright. "I'd like to pay you back. Michael told

25

me your help quit last week. So I thought maybe I could help out for a while. You wouldn't have to pay me much," I added quickly.

Mrs. Cartwright hesitated. "Frankly, I was looking for someone older," she said at last.

"I've got references," I said. "I worked at a camp back home. And my dad and Helen won't need me much until the inn opens next month."

"Well, I can certainly use the help," Mrs. Cartwright said, considering the situation, "I can only pay minimum wage."

"That's fine with me. Does that mean I have the job?"

Mrs. Cartwright nodded. "You can start on Monday."

I felt great. The job was exactly what I needed: it would give me something to do with my time, keep me away from the inn and Helen's too-cheery attitude, and put me closer to whatever social life this mountain had to offer. It also, not coincidentally, gave me the chance to spend time with Michael.

"Oh, thank you, thank you, Mrs. Cartwright," I said as we walked back into the store. "You won't regret this, I promise."

"Regret what?" Michael asked, looking up from the register.

"Isn't it wonderful, Michael?" Mrs. Cartwright said. "Anna's going to fill in at the store until school starts."

Michael nodded in my direction, then walked toward the rear of the store. As he passed, I noticed a strange expression on his face I couldn't decipher with certainty, but it made me shudder. I had the awful feeling Michael wasn't too pleased with his mother's decision.

Chapter Three

My fear about Michael was confirmed on my first day on the job. Well, sort of confirmed. Michael said hello to me when I walked in, but throughout the rest of the morning he kept to himself, barely answering my questions about the stock and store procedures. It was pretty clear that he didn't like the idea of a stranger working in the store.

One good thing did happen that day. I met Cass Santiago. She had run into the store for a pack of chewing gum around noon and was surprised to see me behind the cash register.

"Who're you?" she asked. She was almost as tall as I am, with long, silky black hair that was tied back in a braid.

"Anna. My folks just bought the old Turner house. I'm working here for the summer."

"Great, new blood," she said. Her warm smile made me feel welcome. "Doing anything for lunch?"

When I told her I had no plans she insisted I meet her at Carlyle's Luncheonette next door.

Fifteen minutes later I was sitting at one of the restaurant's old Formica tables, listening to Cass giving me the rundown on life at Blue Mountain. Like me, she'd be a junior at Blue Mountain High in the fall, along with fifty others.

"Wow, some of my classes in Rutherford were nearly that big," I told her.

"Didn't you get lost in the crowd?" she wondered.

"At first," I admitted. "When I was a freshman it took me nearly an entire day to find the gym. And it didn't help when some big-shot senior told me to take the elevator."

Cass looked at me blankly.

"There wasn't any elevator," I explained.

She laughed. "Well, I don't think you'll have any trouble finding your way around our school. And I'm really glad you're here. Sometimes it gets boring seeing the same kids year after year."

"I was afraid of that," I mumbled as I took a sip of my soda.

"It'll be different for you. Everyone will be new," Cass said. "And the good thing about this place is that everyone knows everyone else. Nobody feels like a stranger."

This was the opening I was waiting for. "So you know Michael Cartwright?"

Cass nodded as her eyes fixed on her cheeseburger. "It's such a shame about him."

"His blindness, you mean?" I tried to keep my voice even, not wanting to sound too curious.

She nodded again. "He had so much going for him."

"You mean he hasn't always been blind?"

"Oh, no," Cass said in a hushed whisper. She leaned over the table, apparently not wanting anyone else in the crowded restaurant to hear her. "He was in a terrible accident last February. Some drunk slammed into the car he was in."

I felt my chest tighten. "It hasn't even been six months. . . ."

"And to make matters worse," Cass went on, "Michael hardly ever leaves the store now."

"I guess it's hard to get around when you can't see."

"It's not like we haven't tried," Cass said, a trace of exasperation in her voice. "All his friends have been around, practically begging him to come out. But he just refuses."

"Sounds like he's scared. I saw a TV show once about this girl who got paralyzed and didn't want to be around her old friends. Turned out she was afraid how they'd react."

Cass eyed me curiously. "Maybe you can help."

"Me?" I nearly dropped my fork. "Why me?"

"Because Michael doesn't know you," Cass said. "You're the one person who can't compare him with what he was. Maybe he'll listen to a stranger. My mom told me that sometimes it's easier to take advice from someone you don't know."

I didn't think about Cass's suggestion again until the next morning, when two tall, athletic-looking guys entered the store. I was standing in the hardware section sorting out the bins of screws that had been messed up earlier by a group of little kids, so the boys didn't see me. But I watched with interest as they approached Mrs. Cartwright at the front counter. "Where's Michael?" asked the one with the curly blond hair.

Mrs. Cartwright smiled and then shook her head, as if she had been through this routine dozens of times before. "Good morning, Les, Bobby. Michael's out back in the stockroom."

The hardware section was in the back of the store, so I was able to watch as Les punched Michael's arm playfully. "Hey, you hermit, how's it going?"

I winced at his teasing, but Michael just shrugged. "Fine," he said.

"You missed a great game yesterday," Bobby, the other boy, said. "Mr. Boomer here, Les, hit a homer clear into Hanleys' tomato patch. Boy, was the old man mad, the ball knocked down one of his biggest plants."

"Not half as mad as I was," Les said. "I had to get the ball—all covered with pulp and juice. A mess." He chuckled a little as he leaned over and draped an arm around Michael's shoulder. "But I didn't come to talk about the game." He lowered his voice, and I couldn't make out the rest of what he said. All I heard was something about a party.

"Another one of your victory blowouts?" Michael asked.

"Everyone was there," Bobby said. "Even the Bliss twins." He puckered his lips as if imagining a girl in front of him. "We partied until midnight."

Les nodded. "It would have gone longer, but Jill Mahoney's dad came by and broke it up."

"Typical Mahoney," Michael said. "Remember last fall when he told us we were too old to go trick-or-treating?"

"And slammed the door in our faces?" Bobby laughed. "We had a great time that night, didn't we?"

"Yeah, we all ended up at Lisa's house." Suddenly the smile disappeared from Michael's face, and the other boys grew strangely silent, their eyes fixed on the floor.

Finally Bobby spoke up. "Last night, Cartwright, was the best party of the summer. You should have been there."

Michael pulled away from the others. "You know I couldn't come," he said gruffly.

"Why not?" Bobby asked.

"I just can't."

"We're continuing the party tomorrow night at my house," Bobby said, deliberately ignoring him. "Be there at eight."

"Forget it," Michael said, backing away slightly.

"I could drive you over," Les offered.

"Will you just lay off me?" Michael's voice had turned cold and angry.

"You've got to get out sometime, man," Bobby pleaded.

"Time's running out," Les added. "School starts in a few weeks. What're you going to do then?"

"I'm not going back," Michael said. "You know that."

Bobby turned to Les. "Come on, Boomer, let's cut out of here. We're wasting our time."

"You're right. If this turkey wants to spend the rest of his life counting soup cans, who are we to stop him?" Les walked a few steps then stopped and turned. "See ya around, Cartwright."

My eyes stayed on Michael as the boys left. I saw him bite his lip and take a few deep breaths. I could only imagine what he was feeling. His conversation with Les and Bobby confirmed what Cass had told me: Michael had cut himself off from his friends—and was miserable. Maybe Cass was also right about my being able to help him.

Back in Rutherford I don't think I would have had the nerve to do what I did next. But I was in a new town, dealing with new people. Michael had gotten about two degrees friendlier since the day before. I hoped he wouldn't hate me for what I was about to do. I went back to the storeroom and rapped on the side of the wall. "Knock, knock, it's me," I called.

Michael looked up from the box he was opening. "Hi, Anna." His voice was flat, emotionless. "What do you want?"

"Who were those boys?"

"Les and Bobby? Just some guys."

"Oh," I said. "How come you didn't introduce me?"

"I'm sorry. I never thought about it."

"You know," I said, choosing my words carefully, "it's tough moving to a new town, not knowing anybody. I feel really alone, out of place.

And then," I went on with mock indignation, "when somebody my age finally comes into the store you don't even have the common courtesy to introduce me."

Michael flashed me a grin. "I promise I won't do it again. But don't worry. School will be starting soon, and you'll make plenty of friends there."

"I don't want to wait until school starts," I told him. "What about that party they were talking about?"

"You little snoop!" he said with a laugh. "Actually, the party's a good idea. You'll meet everyone there. I'll give you Bobby's address."

I took a deep breath. "Would you take me, Michael?" I had never asked a boy out before. Instantly, I saw I'd made a mistake. His face was dark with anger.

"Forget it, Anna. I'm not going."

"Why?"

"Isn't it obvious?" he asked.

Anyone with the least amount of common sense would have let the conversation die its natural death right there, but somehow I couldn't give up. "The only thing that's obvious to me is that you've got a lot of friends who care about you and miss having you around," I told him. "And I think you miss them, too."

36

Michael took a deep breath. "I think," he said, "you ought to get back to work in the store."

"I'm just trying to help you!"

"You want to help?" He jeered. "Then leave me alone!"

"So you can sit here and feel sorry for yourself?"

"Look," he said, obviously trying to control his temper, "it's very nice of you to want to help me. I appreciate it. But there isn't anything you or Bobby or Les or anyone else can do. And another thing, I don't need a lecture on feeling sorry for myself from someone who doesn't know what she's talking about. You can't possibly understand what it's like being blind. So, please, Anna, just leave me alone." With that he turned and was gone.

I stood there feeling sick to my stomach. Not only had I failed to draw Michael out of his shell, I'd gotten him so mad he'd probably never speak to me again.

Mrs. Cartwright called me back into the store, which had suddenly become crowded with a busload of kids from a nearby day camp. Michael and I worked side by side all that day. And I was right. He didn't say a single word to me.

The next morning I entered the store with a feeling of dread. I'd spent most of the night awake, replaying the awful scene with Michael. Now, I wasn't looking forward to more of the silent treatment—which was exactly what I got. Finally, after lunch I decided that I couldn't take it any longer. Michael was working in the back of the store. Summoning all my courage, I went up to him.

"Michael? It's me, Anna."

He turned his head away, as if he didn't want to deal with me.

"You were right," I said. "I didn't have any right to say the things I did. I'm sorry."

He turned back to me but didn't say anything.

All right, I told myself, *you've done what you could. If he can't accept an apology, that's his problem.* I made my way back toward the front of the store.

"Anna, wait!" he called suddenly. "Would you come back here for a moment?"

"Why should I?" I asked, close to tears.

"Because—because I want to apologize, too. I shouldn't have snapped at you like that. I'm sorry." He held out his hand to me. "Friends?"

"Friends." I put my hand in his and felt its warmth and strength. "There's just one thing—"

"I told you I don't want to go to the party," he said warily.

"Not that. How about showing me around town?"

"There's not much to see."

"There's got to be something besides this store and Carlyle's. Some place you like to hang out?"

Michael thought for a moment. "Well, there's the pond."

"A pond? Maybe we can go there for our lunch hour someday when it's slow. Have a picnic, or even go fishing. I love to fish. My dad used to take me to Huntington Beach to fish off the pier." I knew I was rambling again, but I was anxious to get a response, any response but the dull, expressionless stare I was seeing.

"There aren't any fish in the pond," he answered after a long pause. "Only ducks. At least I still think they're there. I haven't—seen the pond in a long time."

"So let's find out," I begged. "I don't want to have to find this pond by myself."

It seemed like an eternity before Michael answered. "Okay," he said. "I'll take you—so long as no one else is around."

We had our picnic the following Tuesday. That was the slowest day of the week, and Mrs. Cartwright was able to handle the store without us. In fact, she was so happy I'd managed to get Michael out of the store that she donated the picnic basket. I packed the lunches myself; well,

Grandma helped, too, by frying the chicken and making her incredibly delicious potato salad.

The truth was, I probably could have found the pond on my own. The trail was a worn, winding path through a dense growth of evergreens and wild grasses that was very easy to follow. Still, I held on to Michael's hand as we made our way slowly toward the clearing. Several times I had to pull away low-growing branches before Michael bumped into them, and he was so unsteady on his feet he took tiny, shuffling steps like an old man. I couldn't help feeling sorry for him, but at the same time I knew I was growing more and more attracted to him. Just holding hands sent this crazy little shiver of excitement through me. And after a while Michael seemed to gain confidence and began to walk with more even, normal strides.

At last we broke through the brush and stood in the beautiful, sunny clearing. There were wildflowers, pink and purple and bright yellow, growing everywhere. The pond glistened in the sun, its dark blue waters dotted with wild ducks.

I wondered what Michael was thinking. He had barely spoken since we left the store. "There's nobody here but us ducks," I said, making a quacking sound, and for the first time that afternoon I saw him smile.

I also noticed beads of perspiration on his

forehead. I couldn't believe he was hot—it was an unusually cool day for August. "Are you all right?" I asked.

"Fine," he assured me as we continued on toward the pond. "I just hadn't realized what it'd be like to be so far from the house and store. Do you know what I mean?"

If I lived to be one hundred, I would never truly understand his fear. The closest I was able to come was to recall the night I was in a restaurant bathroom when somebody turned out the lights by accident. In the blackness everything was strange to me, and it seemed like an eternity before I fumbled my way to the wall switch and turned the lights back on. He had to live with that kind of darkness every day.

I found a good flat spot on which to spread out our blanket. I led Michael to it, and we sat down. He smiled as I handed him his plate. "So I was right about the ducks," he said.

"They're beautiful. Whoops, there goes one," I said as a single bird flapped its wings over the water.

"Funny, I can remember the brown-and-white wings with the green rings around their necks. And that awful quacking." He smiled again as he dug into the potato salad. "Thanks for bringing me here."

"Uh-huh. Thank *you*," I told him. "I couldn't have found this place without you." I sighed. "It's really pretty."

"If you like it now, just wait until winter. It's completely different. The ducks are gone, and the pond freezes, and the ice skaters take over. Do you skate?"

It was the first somewhat-personal question he'd asked me. "Believe it or not we had a rink in Rutherford. I'm not great, but I can get around the ice. What about you?"

"I used to—" His voice grew heavy.

"And you can again," I insisted.

"Maybe." He paused, then said, "If the operation works."

"What operation?"

He put down the chicken. "That's right. You don't know. I'm going to see a surgeon in Los Angeles next month. He thinks he may be able to restore my sight with an operation. They use some kind of sophisticated laser technique."

"Really?" I could hardly believe it.

"I wouldn't joke about something like that."

"So what're you waiting for? You must be going crazy."

"I am." He sighed deeply, as if debating whether to tell me more. "It's the money," he admitted. "We're not rich, and an operation like that costs a ton of money. This is really hard on

42

my mom. . . . Tell me how it looks now," he said, abruptly changing the subject. "Are the three birches still on the right side of the water? Is there still a thick clump of high grass behind the rocks?" He turned to me suddenly, his dark, sightless eyes searching mine. "Oh, Anna, I'd give anything to see it all again!"

Before I could stop him, he stood up and headed toward the pond, stumbling yet moving surprisingly fast. I went after him, caught his wrist, and he stopped, motionless.

"Michael—" I didn't say anything else. Tears filled his eyes, but he blinked them back. I didn't really know what to do, but I put my hand on his shoulder and stroked it gently. "It's only a couple of weeks, Michael. You'll see it again. You'll see it all."

"There's no guarantee."

No guarantee. The words hung in the air as clearly as the rain clouds that had begun to gather. "You mean that you could undergo the operation and still be blind?" I asked.

He shrugged. "It's what they call an 'experimental procedure.' So far, it's only worked in about half the cases. I've just got to be one of the lucky ones."

"You will," I said, thinking for the first time that it was wrong for Michael to get his hopes up. Maybe what he should have been doing was learning to accept his blindness. But who was I to tell him otherwise?

Still a stranger, I realized as our picnic conversation turned to more mundane topics such as the store and the Blue Mountain winter. But if I had my way, we wouldn't be strangers for long.

Chapter Four

About halfway between the inn and the Cartwrights' store, there's a lookout on the road. It's probably the most scenic point on Blue Mountain. You can stand there and look west, clear across the valley. And when the sun's setting, as it was that day after our picnic, it seems as if the whole mountain and valley are lit with a golden red light. It's a good place to be when you need to think things out, and on that particular day I had a lot to think about—mainly Michael Cartwright. So instead of going straight home, I sat down on the stone bench and tried to sort things out.

Because we spent so much time alone in the store, I'd begun to feel as if Michael and I were in our own separate world. In a way, at the store we were, but being with him at the pond had made me realize that if we were ever to have a real relationship, we'd have to deal with the rest of the world. And that's where the trouble began.

The first problem was, of course, Michael's blindness. I'd put off thoughts of dating him because of it. Michael was obviously uncomfortable when he left the store. He'd never even have come to the pond if there'd been other people there. I couldn't imagine doing the things that regular couples do, like going to the movies or football games or dancing. We couldn't even do the very simple thing I happened to be doing at that moment; I might persuade Michael to sit at the lookout with me, but we'd never be able to watch a sunset together.

Unless, of course, the operation worked. And Michael had said it only worked about half the time. I forced myself to be completely honest. What would I do if the operation didn't work and Michael was blind for good? Should I try to make him fall in love with me, anyway, and just get used to having a blind boyfriend? Or should I give up and find someone normal and uncomplicated? Back in Rutherford, Tommy Preston had been everything I thought I wanted—good-looking, outgoing, and a very nice guy. A month before I would have said I was crazy about him, and now that seemed impossible. In fact, the idea of going out with anyone except Michael seemed impossible. With a little shiver I realized that deep down Michael's blindness didn't matter to me. All I knew was that I wanted to be with him.

It was strange, but once Michael told me about his operation hardly a day passed that I didn't hear about it from one person or another. I learned that the reason Mrs. Cartwright drew Xs over the days in the calendar behind the cash register was because it brought her that much closer to September fifteenth, the day she and Michael would be meeting with the surgeon. I also learned that it was the hot topic of conversation around Blue Mountain.

"All his friends know," Cass told me a few days after my picnic with Michael. We were sitting in Carlyle's again. This time Cass had brought along Laura Workman, who'd also be in my new class. With her short blond hair and friendly disposition, Laura reminded me a lot of my best friend, Susan, from Rutherford.

"Michael's been living for that operation," Laura added. "Frankly, I think he's setting himself up for a big disappointment."

"I know," I said. "If the operation works, that would be great, but in the meantime there's so much he could be doing."

"Like what?" Laura wondered. "It's easy for us to talk. We can still see. Michael's life changed forever the night of the accident. He can never go back to what he was. If I were him, I'm not sure I'd act differently. I wouldn't want to get used to blindness."

"How can you say that?" I asked.

"Easy. Before the accident Michael was one of the most popular kids at Blue Mountain—on the football team, hockey, the student government, the honor roll. He had everything going for him. Then, bam! In one night it's all gone."

"No it's not," I insisted. "I know it sounds corny, but he's still alive. And that's what really counts."

"He's only as alive as he wants to be," Cass said matter-of-factly. "After the accident, everything he really wanted was gone."

"What actually happened?" I asked. "I haven't had the nerve to ask him about the accident."

"It was horrible," Laura began. "Jake Taylor was driving home from the Valentine's Day dance at school. It had snowed earlier, and the roads were a mess, so Jake was being extra careful. I know because he'd just gotten his driver's license and had borrowed his dad's car and didn't want to blow his chance of getting it again. But just as they were pulling away from the traffic light on Bolton Road, a drunk driver ran the light and hit them broadside. Jake and Doreen were lucky. They walked away with hardly a scratch. Lisa and Michael weren't so lucky."

"Who's Lisa?" I asked, remembering the awkward silence that had followed the mention of her name the day Les and Bobby had come to the store.

"Michael's girlfriend," Laura answered.

"Oh." It hadn't occurred to me that Michael had a girlfriend. Maybe that, too, accounted for the distance between us. "Uh, I'd better be going," I said, excusing myself from the table. The mood had grown too somber, and I had so much more to think about. So Michael had been a school hotshot—and had had a girlfriend. His world really had been turned upside down. No wonder he wanted to hide from it all.

Chapter Five

"You and Michael will have to run the place today," Mrs. Cartwright told me a few days later. "I have to sign some loan papers down at the bank." *For the operation*, were the words she didn't have to add.

Mrs. Cartwright left me instructions for the shipment of canned goods and the dairy's delivery, but I knew Michael was capable of handling almost everything in the place by himself. She waved goodbye, grabbed the truck keys from the hook, and drove off into the morning drizzle.

There were almost no customers that morning. The temperature had dropped amazingly fast, and it seemed as if everyone had decided to stay indoors. I shivered in my thin summer blouse. Michael sensed my discomfort, made his way to the apartment through the back of the store, and brought out his mother's green sweater for me.

"I can't believe this weather," he said, pulling on a sweatshirt. "It feels like fall." With that, a bolt of lightning shot through the sky and a crash of thunder tore through the mountains.

Looking up at the ceiling, I shuddered. "I thought that was going to tear off the roof."

He laughed. "That's one thing you'll have to get used to. Thunderstorms up here are the worst."

"Fire and brimstone?" I looked out at the rain, now coming down in torrents.

"Something like that." Michael chuckled softly.

"I wish your mother hadn't gone out today." I sat down on the rocking chair, pulling the sweater tighter around me. "The roads must be dangerous."

He nodded and walked over to the Franklin stove. "She's a good driver. If things get really bad, she'll stay at her sister's for a while. How about a fire, Anna? It's really cold in here."

It sounded great to me. In minutes the old Franklin stove roared with heat. We sat on the hooked rug in front of it enjoying the glow, shelling peanuts and talking, knowing full well we wouldn't have to bother with customers. No one in their right mind would be out now.

Suddenly there was another huge crash of

thunder and more lightning. It had come too close this time, and a second later the lights went out. I grabbed Michael's arm. "The electricity went off!" I shouted.

Michael remained calm. "Let's go and see if it hit us," he said. "We'll check the back rooms first." He stood up and held out his hand to me. "I'll be your guide."

"My guide?"

He laughed. "I'm used to the dark, remember? Check everything here in the store, though. If it hit us, there could be a fire."

I knew where the candles were stocked, so with Michael leading the way, we found them first. Then I checked the back of the store. The lightning bolt had seemed close, but on careful inspection I couldn't find anything wrong. I returned to find Michael sitting by the stove, not at all uncomfortable for the lack of electricity.

The three candles I had placed on the long counter and the two on a table by the stove gave the store a rosy, warm glow. Now the boxes stacked along the back wall, leaning against one another in the dark shadows, seemed to be ghostly creatures hovering in the flickering of the candlelight.

I sat down beside him on the rug, and we resumed shelling the roasted peanuts.

"This is fun," I said as I popped another peanut into my mouth. "I haven't had peanuts in the shell since my dad took me to a Rams game last fall. Actually, sitting here in the rain, with the fire, reminds me a lot of the fall."

"It'll be here soon," Michael said wistfully. I thought he was thinking about the days to his operation, but his next words proved me wrong. "I can't tell you how many Sunday afternoons I sat around this stove, shelling peanuts, watching football on TV with—" He cut himself short, and for a moment I thought he might have choked on a nut.

"Michael?" I said.

He sighed deeply. "I'm all right," he said a moment later. "I was just thinking about an old friend."

"Lisa?" I ventured timidly.

He nodded. "You've heard of her?"

"Cass and Laura told me about her," I said. I shuddered as another round of thunder and lightning crashed around us. "I'm sorry, Michael. She should have treated you better."

Michael looked as if a bolt had hit him. "What do you mean?"

"Abandoning you after the accident," I explained.

"She didn't," he said softly.

"Well, I haven't seen her around here. I mean, just because you're blind, that's no reason—"

"No." Michael cut me off. "You've got it wrong. Lisa is dead, Anna. She died in the accident."

"Oh, Michael, I'm so sorry. I didn't know." Without thinking about it I put my arms around him, and to my surprise his arms went around me, holding me with an intensity that took my breath away.

For a while neither one of us talked. I concentrated on the steady pounding of the rain on the roof. And then on the pounding of my heart.

Suddenly the darkness made me bold. "What was she like, Michael?"

He answered unhesitatingly, his arms still strong around me. "What was she like? Little—in height I mean, with long blond hair and the wildest blue eyes. We were good friends. I could talk to her about anything, and she always knew how to make me laugh."

I waited for him to talk more about Lisa, but he surprised me with his next question. "What color is your hair? And your eyes?"

The lights suddenly flicked on, and I jumped back, releasing myself from his arms. "The power's back on! I guess I'd better get back to counting the jam jars."

Michael hadn't moved. "What are they like?" he asked.

"What?"

"Your hair. Your eyes."

I touched my dark unruly hair. In the light I felt strangely awkward with him, especially now that I realized how deeply he had cared about Lisa. And there was no mistaking his tone when he spoke about her—he still missed the girl with the long blond hair and wild blue eyes. It was suddenly very clear to me that whether or not Michael ever regained his sight, I wanted him to care about me the way he had cared about Lisa. Still, that was no excuse for what I said next. "I guess you could say my hair is on the light side," I lied. "And my eyes are sort of blue."

I watched his mouth curl into a soft smile. Obviously I'd said the right thing.

Chapter Six

For the next hour or so I busied myself with the list of things Mrs. Cartwright had left for me to do. Not one customer came into the store to give me a break from the tedious counting and log entering. While I worked in the store, Michael was busy doing a few chores for his mom in the back rooms.

At three-thirty Mrs. Cartwright called to say she'd be staying at her sister's until the rain slowed. She promised to be home by five-thirty and asked me to wait there until she arrived.

I called Grandma so that she wouldn't worry, and she said she'd hold dinner for me. Helen and my father had gone to Los Angeles to pick up some lamps and wouldn't be back until the next day, so it would only be the two of us anyway. Which didn't matter, I told myself. Helen and my father had been so busy since we moved that I barely saw them when they were there.

When I finally finished my work, I made a pot of tea. Michael pulled a package of cookies off the shelf, and we took a break at the kitchen table.

"How long has your mother had to run the store by herself?" I asked.

Michael stirred his tea in deep thought. "Since my dad died. I was four, but I can remember him . . . just as you can remember your mother, I guess. He was very sick for a long time."

Why was it that every question I asked led to a painful memory? I turned the conversation to something more positive. "I'll bet you've made lots of plans for after the operation."

He smiled as I filled his cup with tea. "Uh-huh. If everything turns out okay, I'll go back to school and finish. I really want to graduate with my class."

I knew that much already. Mrs. Cartwright had told me that Michael had passed a special exam last June so he wouldn't fall behind the others.

"When will you be able to go back?"

He shook his head. "A month—six weeks, maybe. I'll have a lot of catching up to do."

"Can't you study at home?"

He shrugged. "I'd need a tutor—and they cost money."

"Not necessarily," I said. "I could help you. I could pick up your homework and then hand it in the next day. Like a tutor—or at least a helper of sorts."

He tilted the chair back and sighed deeply. "I couldn't ask you to do that. It'd be an awful lot of work."

"I could do it, Michael. Consider it a kind of selfish gesture on my part. By the time I go through my senior year, I'll be way ahead because I'll have done it all with you." I laughed. "See, I'm really just thinking of myself!"

He smiled and then broke into a laugh. I joined him. It felt good to see him so happy and relaxed. Then he reached out his hand to touch mine. "It was a lucky day for me when you walked into our store."

Remembering the day made me smile. "Want to know a secret?"

"What?" he asked.

"I thought you were stuck-up," I told him, laughing. "When you didn't look at me when we were introduced, I thought you were a snob!"

Michael's laughter stopped. "I'm sorry, Anna."

"No problem," I said lightly, trying to recapture the mood. "Let's see, we were talking about your future. So what's going to happen after high school?" I asked, pouring my second cup of tea.

He shrugged. "My dad left a college fund for me. It isn't much, but it's enough to get started. My mother guards it with her life—she won't touch it for anything. Anyhow, I think I want to do something with computers. I've always been crazy about them."

"So that's your dream?"

"Everyone up here on Blue Mountain has a dream," he said, brushing the crumbs from the tablecloth into his open palm. "Most of them dream of getting off the mountain, but my real dream is just to *see* the mountain again."

I could understand that. I picked up the teacups to wash them.

"What about you, Anna? What's in your future?" He stood directly behind me at the sink.

Carefully I put the cups and saucers on the counter. The liquid detergent I squirted into the dishpan exploded into bubbles when I turned on the hot water. "Oh, college in two years, for starters. I'd really like to be a fashion designer."

"Any other dreams?"

"Truthfully?"

"Truthfully."

I turned off the water and spun around to look into his sightless dark eyes. They seemed to be searching my soul. "I want to go back to Rutherford."

"Don't you like it here?"

I turned back to the sink. "Oh, I like the store and working here with you and your mom, but I still miss Rutherford. I had my school, my friends." I sighed. "I could go back now and live with my aunt Ivy but my dad won't let me."

Michael grabbed the dish towel, then picked up a cup from the dish rack. "He doesn't want you to leave?"

I snorted. "He's so busy with the inn he hardly knows I'm around. Anyhow, he's so happy with Helen, I don't think he'd miss me at all."

Michael felt for the cupboard and carefully stacked the cup in its place. "I'm not so sure," he said, shaking his head. "I bet Helen would miss you, too."

"I doubt it," I replied. "They'll open the inn soon, and she'll be so busy she won't have time to miss anyone." I spilled out the dishwater. "Grandma would miss me a little. But then she'll be busy in her kitchen."

"I'd miss you," he said suddenly. "I'd miss you terribly." He reached out and touched my arm.

Suddenly the bell over the screen door in the store warned us that someone had entered. "I'm home," Mrs. Cartwright called out in her cheery voice. "It's stopped raining at last!"

Chapter Seven

Almost two weeks later I stood in front of the nearly finished inn, my arms wrapped inside the blue oversize sweater I wore over my stone-washed jeans. It wasn't just the early-morning cool air that was making me shiver. It was the nervous tension that made me shift anxiously from foot to foot as I waited for the school bus to come up the hill. It was the first day of school, and I wished it were already over.

I hated the idea of having lots of people stare at me, the new girl in school. Yet at the same time I was excited about making new friends. Now that I knew Michael liked me and that Cass and Laura had become my friends, I'd begun to feel welcome here. I knew I wouldn't be lonely, but I still missed Rutherford, especially after having talked to my friend Susan the night before.

Over breakfast Helen had tried to convince me that in a few short days I'd feel as if I'd always gone to Blue Mountain High. I found that a little hard to believe. I think she'd finally realized how hard the move had been on me and was feeling a little bit guilty.

My tension began to ease as soon as the school bus arrived. Cass was already on board and waved her arms to get my attention as soon as I stepped inside. We compared schedules, and I was relieved to see we had the same government, English lit, and French classes.

"Remember, there aren't as many of us here," Cass reminded me. "By the end of the week you ought to know the whole school."

I had to hand it to Cass. She really went out of her way to get me into the swing of things. We had a few minutes to kill before homeroom, and she insisted on giving me a rush tour of the school. Not that the tour would have taken long, anyway. Blue Mountain was a small, two-story stucco building about a quarter the size of Rutherford High. The place was teeming with kids, and as we made our way down the first floor hall Cass stopped repeatedly to introduce me to my classmates. The names went by in a blur, but everyone smiled and said they were glad to meet me, and I took that as an encouraging sign.

The biggest surprise for me that morning was the lack of any surprises. The classes went on much as they did at Rutherford—being up in the mountains didn't make the teachers any less boring. My English teacher even assigned us an essay, which was exactly what my old English teacher had done on the first day of school the year before.

The school was small enough for everyone to share the same lunch period. I met Cass and Laura at a corner table in the cafeteria. We sat next to a window that overlooked the athletic field, where a few members of the football team were practicing. Cass reintroduced me to two of the girls I'd met that morning—Kelly Bruce and Jill Mahoney.

"Glad you're here. I just ask one thing," Jill said. "Keep your hands off Kenny Thompson. He's mine." She pointed outside to the football players, but I couldn't tell which one he was.

Cass grinned as she put down her milk. "You don't have to worry about Anna. She's got a boyfriend."

I felt my face flush. Cass was jumping to conclusions, to put it mildly. Much as I would have liked it, Michael wasn't exactly my boyfriend. "No, I don't," I said.

Kelly nudged my arm with her elbow. "Go on, you look like you're hiding something. Who's the lucky guy?"

When I didn't answer, Cass filled them in: "Michael Cartwright."

Kelly's eyebrows shot up. "Really," she said. "I thought he was out of circulation—permanently."

"Because he's blind?" I asked.

"Well—uh, no," Kelly stammered, embarrassed by the directness of my question.

"So what's it like to date him?" Jill asked.

"I haven't," I answered. "I've spent the past few weeks working at his mother's store. We've gotten to be good friends, but that's all it is."

"Yeah, I know what you mean. I could never date a blind guy," Kelly continued. "Too bad about Michael, though. He was really a hunk."

I wanted to say he still *is*, but I didn't want to keep the conversation going. It was getting too personal—the idea of being Michael's girlfriend was something I wasn't ready to discuss.

But Laura wouldn't let the subject drop. "He still could be a hunk. He's got that operation coming up, you know."

"I'd be surprised if he ever dates again," Jill said. "Even if he *could* see."

"Why's that?" I asked.

The table grew eerily quiet, as if some spirit had suddenly hovered over it. In a way, one had. "Doesn't she know about Lisa?" Kelly asked Cass anxiously.

"Michael told me about her," I said calmly. "That they had been good friends since they were kids."

Kelly pursed her lips for a second. Finally she said, "They were a lot more than that."

"You mean they dated?" I said the words matter-of-factly, but they left a strange taste in my mouth. "I knew that."

"They were the primo couple around here," Kelly told me. "Jake Taylor used to joke about needing a crowbar to pry them away from each other. They were inseparable."

"Yeah, everyone was taking bets on when they'd marry—one or two weeks after graduation," Jill said.

"They were that close?" I could hardly say the words.

Kelly nodded. "Michael couldn't bear to talk about her for a long time after the accident."

"It's still hard to believe it happened," Jill said. "Even now, every time I ride by that intersection a little shiver goes down my spine."

I knew what she meant. I was feeling goose bumps myself while she spoke. Now that I knew the full truth about Lisa, a lot of things about Michael were starting to make more sense. He probably still loved her, and for all I knew, always would. Maybe my feelings for him were hopeless, and we could never be more than good friends.

That night I sat and stared at my image in the oval vanity mirror. All I'd been able to think about since lunch was Michael, yet my thoughts were so jumbled I felt paralyzed. His blindness was something I thought I could deal with. But now I realized there was an even bigger problem—Lisa. I'd wanted to believe that she hadn't meant that much to him, that the sadness I saw on his face when he had mentioned her was the sadness anyone would feel when remembering a friend who'd died. But if they were really as close as Kelly had said, Michael wouldn't be interested in starting a new relationship—even with his sight back. Lisa might be dead, but Michael still loved her.

There was another problem, too—a minor one compared with Lisa, but one that I had caused and couldn't stop thinking about. I'd lied to Michael. I'd let him believe I looked like Lisa. Now as I pulled a brush through my dark, unruly hair I sighed. Even if I bleached my hair to Lisa's color I was still stuck with very unblue brown eyes. And I couldn't bear the thought of Michael's finding out what I really looked like.

To begin with he'd know I had lied to him. And even if he could get past that, would he ever be attracted to me when, in fact, I looked like the exact opposite of the girl he'd really fallen in love with? I'd lied because I wanted Michael to imagine me as being as beautiful as Lisa. I'd wanted him to fall in love with me. And now the lie itself almost guaranteed that would never happen.

Crawling under the covers in bed, I turned off the lamp, punched the pillow a few times, and tried to fall asleep. I couldn't, and after a while I grew so restless I crept to my desk and picked up my government textbook. Now, if there was ever a surefire thing to put me to sleep—

Just as I felt myself nod off, there was a knock at my bedroom door. The book slid to the floor as Helen poked her head through the door. "Hi," she said brightly. It had turned cold outside, and she was wearing her pink velvet, winter robe. "I wondered if you'd turned in yet. How'd school go?"

I picked up the book and crawled back into the rumpled bed. "I survived," I told her wearily.

"I knew you would." She reached over to give me a hug. "I'm sorry I didn't get a chance to ask you earlier. With the inn opening on Friday, I'm just a wreck these days."

"I understand," I said, and I did. Though I hadn't even noticed it happening, my anger over the move to Blue Mountain had gradually disappeared.

She put her hand on my arm and rubbed it soothingly, just as she used to do when I was little and had trouble falling asleep. "I know how rough and unfair this move was for you, but you've come through like a real trouper. I'm proud of you, Anna."

Helen had her hair done up in rollers under a pink scarf, but at that moment I thought she was quite beautiful. "Thanks, Helen." I smiled. "You were right about Blue Mountain. It's kind of grown on me."

"I know."

"But how could you? I only realized it today—at school."

"I saw it in your eyes," Helen said, the lines around her own pale eyes crinkling upward as she smiled. "The way you've been talking about that boy at the store."

"Michael." I nodded at her perceptiveness. "I really like him a lot."

"But?" She looked questioningly at me, guessing there was more.

"I think he's still in love with his old girlfriend, Lisa. She died in the accident. I wanted him to like me, so I lied about my looks. When I found out she had blond hair and blue eyes, I—"

Helen guessed the rest. She broke into laughter. "Anna, why on earth would you do such a silly thing? You're pretty the way you are, with that thick dark hair and those lovely eyes! People don't like others just for their appearances!"

Where have you been? I thought. "Helen, you don't know guys today! I hear them talking about girls! There's a lot of competition—maybe it wasn't like that in *your* day."

"Oh, Anna, *my* day wasn't that long ago! Sure, guys turn their heads when a pretty girl goes by—that will never change—but they end up with the girls who are pretty inside, the ones who have character."

I turned my face away from her. "This Lisa must have been really pretty inside, too," I said sadly. "I mean, I can see it in his face when he talks about her. Now he'll be getting his sight back, and he won't like the way I look, and worse, he'll know I lied to him."

Helen bent down and kissed my cheek. I breathed in the faint aroma of her apple blossom perfume. "You'll see," she whispered as she turned off the lamp. "If he likes you now, he'll like you when he can see the real you." She walked to the door and then turned. "Anna, for whatever it's worth, I think you're beautiful." Softly she closed the door behind her.

I could hear her footsteps going down the winding stairs, reaching the second floor landing, and then the fading sounds going down to the first floor. I rolled over in bed, closed my eyes, and tried to drift off, but I couldn't. All I could picture was Michael looking at me for the first time. He was turning away, disappointment in his dark, troubled eyes.

Chapter Eight

The following afternoon I entered the general store and walked as quietly as I could up to the counter. I was carrying a heavy load of books. Michael was behind the cash register, counting out the coins. I knew the bell had alerted him that someone had come in, but I wanted to see if he could tell it was me.

"Pardon me," I said, dropping my voice a few octaves to disguise it. "Where are the candy bars?"

"Over on aisle—" He stopped short, a smile spreading slowly across his face. "Anna, is that you?"

"How could you tell?"

"That perfume you've been wearing lately. It's a dead giveaway."

"One day I'll change it and really mix you up,"

I teased. I was glad he'd guessed who I was so quickly. The books were getting heavy, and I had to put them down before my arms broke. They fell on the counter with a dull thud.

"What's that?" he asked.

"A surprise," I said. "But first I want to tell you about school. I'd have stopped by yesterday to tell you about my first day, but they needed me at the inn."

"You hated it, right?" He leaned over the counter. "The teachers were ogres, and all the kids threw tomatoes at you."

"How'd you guess?" Chuckling, I walked away from him to pick up a pack of mint chewing gum. Then I placed the coins in his hand. He closed it over mine and held it gently. For a moment I was able to forget all about Lisa.

"No kidding, how was it?" he asked.

"Great," I admitted. "Everyone made me feel comfortable. I met an old friend of yours, too, Kelly Bruce."

"The loudmouth?" He grinned. "What sort of gossip was she dishing out?"

The words just blurted out. "She told me about you and Lisa."

Michael closed his eyes, as if to hide the pain he was still feeling. "That's all in the past. It's over," he said. But his expression said otherwise.

I decided to change the subject. "On to the future, right?" I said brightly.

"Right."

"Here's your start, Michael."

"What's this?"

"Your key to graduating with your class. Your textbooks. You can graduate if you turn in all the assignments like everyone else. I'll help you, and so will your mother."

He shot out a hand in protest. "No, I can't do it that way! I have to wait until I go back and *see* what I'm doing." He reached out a hand to me, and I took it to show him I was still right in front of him. "Please, Anna," he said. "Please don't ask me to do this. Anyhow, I don't know how you got those books. I'm not even registered."

"Yes, you are." Mrs. Cartwright came from the back rooms, her face showing concern for her son. "Michael, the day I went to the bank I made the arrangements. You have two people here who want to help you get on with your life—me and Anna. And there are people at the school who want to help, too."

Michael lowered his head, sulking. Mrs. Cartwright and I exchanged glances. "Michael . . ." He raised his voice. "This will give you something to do while you're in the hospital. Your mother can read the books to you and quiz you. If nothing else, it'll make the time pass."

He sighed. "I know it sounds crazy, but this makes me feel like I'm giving into the blindness—

like I'm putting up with it—in case the operation doesn't work."

"Don't even talk like that!" I said. "Of course it'll be a success!" As I finished the words, I looked at Mrs. Cartwright for an encouraging word, but she turned away and began to poke at the candy bars. A sudden chill ran through me. I knew, I always knew, there was no guarantee for Michael.

He reached out and touched the books on the counter. "That was some load to carry."

"I'll say." Feeling encouraged, I ran down the titles. "This is your English literature anthology, and your social studies book. Here's *Psychology*, second edition. This one's *Chemistry Studies for the Senior*." There were three more, and he winced as I read off their titles. "Miss Whitcomb says most of senior year is a rehash of everything you've ever learned. She said you shouldn't have too hard a time because you've always been a good student." Everything I said sounded carefully rehearsed—because it was.

Michael stood there, running his fingers along the bindings of the books. "Take them back," he said abruptly.

"But, Michael—"

"I can't talk now. I just remembered. I've got to unload the cans of soup," he said, heading for the back of the store. "Why did we order so much this time?" he grumbled to himself.

I wanted to run after him, but I wasn't sure what to say. He obviously didn't want to listen, anyway.

The bell jangled as a customer walked into the store. I helped him load up on bananas and oranges and milk, and as he was leaving Michael returned with a box of soup cans. Mrs. Cartwright took over at the register, and I crouched down next to him beside the shelf.

Together we made room for the cans. He unloaded and I stacked. "I'm really mad at you," I said.

"Why?"

"Isn't it obvious? The books."

"Oh, that." He handed me a can. "I don't want to talk about it."

"But I do," I said sharply. "I thought it was all settled that day I offered to bring them home for you."

"I never agreed."

I stood up and stared down at him. "I know what it is. You're plain scared, Michael. You're afraid to try. You'd rather pretend to be helpless than try to make something of yourself. Well, maybe it's easier this way, but in the end you're only cheating yourself."

"Anna"—his voice was tense—"you're not being fair."

"No?" I pulled a sheet of paper out of the back

77

pocket of my jeans. "Here are tonight's assignments. There's not much, really. I could stop by to pick up your homework before my bus comes in the morning if you think you want to take a stab at it." I handed him the paper.

"And here's what I think of that idea." He took it in his hand and crumpled it completely.

"Michael!" Mrs. Cartwright said sharply.

"Stay out of this, Mom," he called. "Look, Anna, I think you'd better leave."

"But, Michael—" My voice was trembling.

"I know you mean well, but I don't need anyone telling me what to do with my life. I'll hit the books when I'm good and ready—and right now I'm not." Kicking aside the box of cans, he got up and headed into the back rooms.

All I could do was stand and look helplessly at Mrs. Cartwright. "Don't worry, Anna," she said soothingly. "I'll try to talk some sense into him. I'm sure he'll calm down in a while."

I wished I were as confident. All I'd wanted to do was help Michael and try to make things better for him. All I'd accomplished, however, was to ruin my best chance of getting closer to him.

Chapter Nine

Helen was waiting for me on the porch when I got home from school the next day. "Where have you been?" she cried, looking unusually anxious.

I didn't know what her problem was. There was no rule that said I had to be home as soon as school ended. "Cass dragged me to this committee meeting," I told her, shrugging. "For the Oktoberfest. It's a real big thing around here."

"Well you'd better turn around and head back to the general store." The words sounded like an order.

"Why?"

"Michael's been calling every five minutes. He wants to see you."

"Did he say why?"

"Something about eating crow?" Helen gave me a puzzled look. "It sounded very important."

She didn't have to tell me that. I ran to get my bike, and less than ten minutes later I was parking it against the side wall of the store.

Mrs. Cartwright, who was busy with a customer at the front counter when I entered, smiled when she saw me. Silently she pointed toward the back rooms and indicated with a nod of her head that that was where I should go.

Michael opened the door before I'd finished knocking. "Anna." He smiled. "I'm glad you came."

"How'd you know—"

"Your perfume. Remember?" He laughed. "Come on in. I've got to talk to you." He led me to an armchair, then sat down opposite me on the sofa. "I owe you a gigantic apology. Again. Can you forgive me for being a dumb jerk?"

I let out a deep breath and relaxed. He didn't hate me, after all. "Maybe," I said.

"I shouldn't have said what I did yesterday. You were right about me. I *am* scared. And having you say so to my face scared me even more." Abruptly Michael got up, walked to the dining room table, and returned with a couple of sheets of paper. He handed them to me. "I may be scared, but I'm not a coward. Here's the homework from yesterday. Would you take it to school for me?"

I stood up and took it from him. "I'd be glad to," I said. "But what made you change your mind?"

He motioned for me to sit down again. "Mom gave me an earful," he admitted. "And I got to thinking about what you said. I *would* be cheating myself if I didn't try. Besides, if I don't start now I'll only be making it harder on myself when I get back from the operation. Why should I give myself that kind of grief?"

"Exactly," I said. "Whoops, excuse me. I don't want to sound like I'm trying to tell you what to do."

"Never mind." He shook his head. "I know you're only trying to help. That's another reason why I wanted you to stop by. I had Mom call the school to get today's homework. Mind lending me a hand?"

"I can't think of anything I'd rather do," I said truthfully.

We started with the chemistry assignment. I felt a bit helpless as I read what to me were indecipherable formulas and watched while Michael struggled to balance them. I bit my lip when, in frustration, he finally flung his pencil across the room. "I can't do these," he said angrily.

I was afraid he was going to tell me to leave again. So I didn't say anything, waiting for his next move. After a while he asked, "Anna, are you still here?"

"Yes."

"I need a break from science," he said, his voice sounding surprisingly calm. "Let's tackle history."

For the next half hour I read from the textbook about the origins of World War I. It was actually pretty interesting. Michael hadn't tried to interrupt me or talk, so I figured he thought so, too. "Okay, now you've got to answer a couple of questions," I said when I got to the end of the chapter.

"You've got a nice voice," he said.

"Huh?" I hadn't expected to hear that.

"Really, you do," he said. "Do you sing?"

"A little," I said, suddenly feeling shy.

"Would you?"

"No way," I told him. There were some things I wouldn't do, even for Michael.

"Well, then I'm not studying."

"Michael, that's not fair!"

"Then you have to do something else," he said with a sly smile.

"What?"

"Come here."

I moved to the couch and sat down next to him. As I read him the questions at the end of the chapter, Michael put his arm around me, and drew me close. I didn't even listen to his answers. Sitting that close to him, I felt so happy I thought I'd melt right into the sofa springs.

That weekend was the grand opening of Willows Inn, which meant that we were really there to stay. There was no going back to Rutherford, and, to my surprise, I realized that didn't seem so terrible. It also meant that the household was in a flurry of activity on Friday morning. All five guest rooms had been reserved, and check-in time was noon.

Grandma had set her hair the night before, and her gray corkscrew curls bounced around her head as she went over the list of last-minute things to do. "Towels and washcloths placed in each bathroom," she mumbled as she ran her fingers down the list.

I grabbed my orange juice, cut a sliver of cinnamon cake, and quickly gulped down the drink.

"All beds made," she went on. "Everything dusted. Guess I'll check the porch to make sure all the rockers are straight."

Helen bumped into her as she entered the kitchen. "They're straight, Lucy. I did it a few minutes ago." My grandmother was very proud of those rockers, as my father had made them himself during the last two frantic weeks. "You take care of the kitchen," Helen said. "I'll be responsible for everything else."

My father walked into the kitchen with the reservation book in his hand. "Helen, did you know we have a honeymoon couple? Let's make sure there are flowers in their room."

"I've taken care of that already," Helen said.

Dad left the kitchen and went to the living room, where he sat down on the sofa by the bay window rechecking the list. I grabbed my books and walked toward him for my hug and kiss. "Have fun, Dad. See you later this afternoon."

As soon as I got on the bus and saw my friends, I forgot all about the excitement at home. Cass and Laura immediately started talking about the Oktoberfest and Halloween Dance. We were on the planning committees for both events, and Laura had come up with an idea for decorating the auditorium. I was barely listening, thinking instead how much fun it'd be going to the dance with Michael. I might have been jumping the gun, but I was hoping he'd ask me. We were getting along great now. I'd been reading to him for three days, and each session had gotten better than the one before. Just thinking about him filled me with a warm, happy feeling.

Laura nudged my arm. "You haven't listened to a word I've said," she complained.

"Yes, I have," I said, lying.

"Then why do you have that goofy look on your face? I just asked you to help me unload a truckful of hay!"

"I'm a little preoccupied," I admitted. "You know, with the inn opening and all."

Cass didn't buy it for a minute. "I know who you were thinking about," she said, teasing me.

"Bobby," I answered with a grin. "I heard he asked you out."

"When he can fit me in around football practice and hanging out with Les and the guys," she said with a sigh. "That comes down to about three hours a week."

"Well, that's more than Eileen Bliss saw of him last year," Laura said optimistically. The two of them then got into a fairly detailed examination of the pros and cons of Bobby as a boyfriend.

I listened to Cass and Laura, secretly relieved that I'd been able to steer the conversation away from Michael. I hadn't let on to anyone that he was a lot more than a friend to me now. It was still too new, and I was still worried that whatever it was we had between us would be over as soon as he saw me for the first time. I knew that in the looks department there was no comparison between ordinary me and the spectacularly beautiful Lisa. All I could imagine was Michael's look of disappointment when he saw what I really looked like—and when he realized I'd lied to him.

The bus pulled up outside school, and I gathered up my books, forcing myself to ignore those thoughts. None of that really mattered, I told myself. The important thing was that Michael was going to see again.

School itself had fallen into a regular, predictable routine. That day we had a quiz in government, I met Cass and Laura for lunch, and my PE teacher made us run around the track four times and I thought I'd collapse from exhaustion. Fortunately, that was my last class, and I was able to recover on the long bus ride home.

As soon as I got off the bus, I saw some of our guests sitting in the rockers on the front porch. It felt weird to see these strangers there, but I was resigned to it being that way from then on.

Politely I said, "Hello," which resulted in having to introduce myself to everyone and ask how they all liked the inn. Everyone seemed pretty content, and one woman even insisted on telling me how the wallpaper in her room reminded her of the house where she had grown up.

As quickly as I could, I escaped to my bedroom with the excuse that I had to do some homework. A few minutes later there was a knock on my door. I opened it to find Helen standing there with a tray of cookies and a glass of milk. It was my usual after-school snack, but I'd hesitated going into the busy kitchen and bothering them that day.

Helen sat down on the bed and sighed. She looked totally frazzled. "Thank goodness we don't have to serve them lunch and dinner. Most of them have made reservations at the Sunburst."

"You look tired," I said.

She sighed again. "I'm trying to make sure they're all happy. Your father says just make sure everything is neat and clean, and the guests will take care of themselves. But I can't help worrying that something will go wrong."

I gave her a quick hug. "Don't worry. Everyone on the porch looked happy and relaxed. You should try to relax, too."

She stood up with a smile. "Thanks, Anna. Come down when you can and help Grandma with our own supper."

"I will," I promised. "I'll be down in just a few minutes as soon as I put away these books and take a shower."

She nodded and left. I showered and dressed quickly. The books were still lying on my bed where I'd thrown them. Slowly I picked them up and stared at one of them, a slim poetry book. It was Michael's and somehow had gotten mixed up with my things. I opened it up and looked at Michael's signature and smiled. I wasn't planning on seeing him till Sunday, the day he was leaving for his operation, but I decided to run over and give him back the book the next day.

Chapter Ten

Getting to see Michael wasn't going to be as easy as I thought. Grandma kept me busy all morning preparing breakfast for our guests. Then I helped seat them and make sure they were all comfortable at the long dining room table. One lady, who was a history teacher, wanted to know what I was studying in school. I must have answered about thirty questions on the Blue Mountain curriculum, which I didn't even know anything about. By the end of breakfast I was dying to get away, though I did my best not to show it. I knew I'd never hear the end of it from Dad and Helen if I was rude to a guest.

Then Helen asked me to make up the beds, while she cleaned the bathrooms. The plan was to scurry in and out of the guest rooms so that all of the guests could enjoy their privacy as much as possible. Following Helen's instructions, I knocked lightly on each door and asked if it was a convenient time to clean the room.

After making the beds it was time to clean all the breakfast dishes and then help Grandma make the biscuits for the following day.

It was going on four-thirty before I could finally grab my bike and escape. Michael was behind the counter when I walked in. He turned as I approached. "Anna?"

"I tried to get over here this morning," I told him, "but there's so much to do since we opened." I handed him his book.

He smiled. "I'm glad you came. I wanted to sit and talk with someone. Mom's busy getting our things ready for the trip, so I'm out here trying to wait on the customers."

There were four more customers, and I pitched in to help. Finally the door closed on the last of them, and I walked over to the burlap bags of peanuts. "I'll buy a bag," I said, trying to make my voice sound bright and cheerful. "If no one else walks in for a while, we can sit on the rug and shell them like old times."

Like a miracle the front door did not open again, and so we settled ourselves on the hooked rug just as we had during the storm, except this time the lights were on. I looked at Michael and felt the pain that hit me in my chest every time I thought about the operation. With luck, I thought, he would see again soon.

"Will you have a private room?"

He shook his head. "No, I'll be in with someone else. But that's better, I think. Not so lonely."

"When will they take the bandages off?"

"Not until the tenth day. They want me to rest a lot." I could see the tension creep onto his face.

Maybe talking about the operation was the wrong thing to do, I thought. I quickly changed the subject. "I forgot to tell you. Mr. James said not to worry about those chemistry problems. No one else could solve them, either."

A customer came in then, and I waited on him while Michael continued to shell peanuts. After he left I resumed my place on the rug and took a few peanuts from Michael's outstretched hand.

"What are you going to do while I'm gone?" he asked suddenly.

"Michael Cartwright, my life doesn't revolve around you," I said, half wishing that it did. "There's school, more work at the inn, and those committees I told you about."

"The Oktoberfest," he said with a smile. "Anna, you're going to love it. They decorate the school with hay and corn and pumpkins, and there's a big festival in town, too."

"We even get a day off from school. My favorite part," I said.

"The Oktoberfest may be fun, but the Halloween Dance is even better. Last year's was really wild. Everyone dressed up in costumes. I wore one of those rubber Dracula masks. It was hotter than anything, but it was worth it. I nearly scared Cass out of her head."

"You? You couldn't scare a butterfly."

"Want to bet? Ask Cass. She still hasn't forgiven me."

"I think I'm glad I missed it," I said.

"Actually I got a little carried away when I did my act for Mrs. Gilchrist."

"The cafeteria cook?"

"She nearly fainted. When she recovered she swore she was going to report me to the principal. She never did, though. But she did get her revenge. The next week we had the worst food in school memory," he said with a laugh. It felt so good to see him so relaxed. I realized it was the first time he'd ever talked at length about the past.

"Anna?" Michael stopped laughing and put out his hand. He touched my arm, his hand sliding down to hold my hand. "Anna, what if it doesn't work? What if I'll never be able to see again?"

"Oh, Michael!" My pain broke through in a

hoarse whisper. "Everything will work out right. I just know it!"

But I didn't know it, I could only hope along with Michael that he would soon be able to see. In the back of my mind, I was scared, too. When he finally came home and saw me—what would happen then? I was so different from his golden girl, Lisa. He had said she was beautiful—and my mirror told me I was not. Just a plain girl, whom no one would ever find special.

I'd promised to help back at the inn, and a quick glance at the clock over the front door told me I'd stayed longer than I should.

I slid my hand from his and stood up. "I have to say goodbye now, Michael." I handed him the lucky coin I'd dug out of my jewelry box just before I rode over to the store. "Here, take this. It's a silly thing—a coin I take to school when I'm going to have a test. I hold it in my hand for good luck."

He took the coin in his fingers and felt the raised good-luck letters. I'd won it at a carnival down in Rutherford one summer. Somehow I'd talked myself into thinking it really was a good-luck charm, even though I knew it was childish and superstitious. It was the only thing I could think of to give him.

Michael stood up, reached for my shoulders, and pulled me close. Then he touched my face, taking it into his hands, and bent down to find my lips. Softly, tenderly, his lips closed over mine, and then he hugged me to him.

"Anna." He breathed into my hair. "Anna . . ."

The bell rang over the door, and I broke away. "Take care," I whispered. "I'll be thinking of you." I left him then and ran toward the door, tears blinding me as I flew through the store and down the cement stairs to my bike.

I couldn't believe it. Michael had kissed me, as if he cared for me the way I cared about him, and there I was crying so hard I could hardly see the road. All I could think about was that if the operation was a success—and Michael was able to see me as I really was—then our very first kiss may very well have been our last.

Chapter Eleven

When I boarded the school bus each morning it was almost empty except for Cass, the Bliss twins, and a few freshmen from my side of the mountain. The day after Michael left I was feeling sorry for him and sorry for me. Sullenly I plopped myself and my books beside Cass.

"Your inn burned down and your father left his wife," she said, trying to imitate my frown. She peered into my eyes curiously. "Right?"

I straightened my skirt underneath me. "Very funny."

"Okay, then what?" she persisted.

"Michael left for L.A. His operation."

"Hmmm," she murmured. "Yeah, that's just awful. I see it now. In no time at all he'll be back on the bus and you'll knock yourself out to sit with him, and then I won't get to sit with you anymore. Yeah, that's bad news, all right!"

Cass usually made me laugh, but that morning I couldn't even smile. As we rode along I concentrated on the trees along the road. Fall came early to Blue Mountain, and the leaves had already begun to change color. I couldn't wait for Michael to see them.

Most of the time Cass wore her long black hair wrapped into a single braid, but that day she wore it loose, falling halfway down her back. Her dark eyes searched mine as she touched my shoulder to swing me around to face her. "Anna, it's going to work out fine."

I sighed. "I guess I'm just a little scared." I couldn't tell her that I'd lied to Michael about my looks and was scared to death I'd lose him after the operation. "Cass, what was Lisa like? I mean, really."

Cass slid down and put her feet on the back of the seat in front of her. "You sure you want to know?"

I nodded. "Tell me the truth."

"Okay." She paused, trying to collect her thoughts. "In one word, I'd say Lisa was gorgeous."

Michael had told me as much, so Cass's words didn't have much effect on me.

"What else?" I pressed on.

"She wanted to be a model, but her parents wouldn't let her. They're sort of stuck-up peo-

96

ple. But Lisa wasn't like that. Everyone liked her."

The bus was starting to fill up, and Cass pulled her feet from the back of the seat. "She was into everything—our drama class, debating, the school paper. And she was pretty smart, too. I don't know how she did it."

"How long was she dating Michael?"

Kids were taking the seats all around us, so Cass lowered her voice. "I guess she and Michael became a couple in their sophomore year. I was just a freshman then, but I always noticed them going through the halls with their heads together. He used to come up behind her and tug on her hair, and then she'd turn around, pretending to be mad, and the next thing you know he'd have his arm around her and they'd be laughing like they had some kind of conspiracy going."

Cass turned to me to see my reaction. "Hey, Anna, if this is hurting you, I'll shut up."

"No," I said. "I want to hear it."

She gave a long sigh. "When the accident happened, I couldn't believe it. Some days I still expect to see her on the bus."

Cass looked down at her books sadly, probably remembering Lisa, while I thought about how hard it must be to lose a friend. We didn't exchange another word during the last few miles to school.

I hadn't really learned anything new about Lisa, except that now I had the image of Michael pulling on her long blond hair, looking into her crystal blue eyes, putting his head close to hers as they carried their books down the hall toward another class. It would be hard for him to forget Lisa, and harder still to fall in love with another girl. Like me.

I went through the rest of the day in a fog, but by three-thirty that afternoon, just before the end of our last class, I regained some of my consciousness. Michael would be in intensive care by then, and back in his own room before long.

Cass met me outside the school bus. "They should have marked you absent today," she said, laughing.

I nodded and joined her in the bus line. "I guess you're right," I agreed. "The hard part's going to be the wait—to see if the operation was successful."

We scrambled into the bus to get our favorite seats in the back. "What do you mean 'if?' Think positively, Anna."

All the way home I thought of Michael in his bed, his head swirled with bandages down to his nose. He was used to the darkness, that wouldn't scare him, but he had to be in some pain after an operation like that. I pictured his mother holding a glass of water for him. I saw tears in her eyes, and suddenly realized I had tears in mine.

By Friday my father, Helen, and Grandma were getting ready for a new set of guests. When I got home that day, several guests had gathered in the living room, where Dad had lit a fire and set up tables for card games.

The phone rang, and I threw my books down on the hall table as I dashed to answer it. My knees went weak when I heard Michael's voice. "Hold on a second," I said, closing the door to shut out the noise from the living room. I returned quickly to the phone. "Michael, how are you? How is everything?" It was so good to hear his voice again. It sounded as if he were right down the road at the general store.

"I'm fine," he answered. "A little anxious for Monday to come—that's when they're going to take off the bandages."

"So soon? Monday? I thought it would be longer than that."

"No. Dr. Story said I'm doing so well there's no need to wait." I could hear him sigh. "Keep your fingers crossed."

"Oh, I will," I promised. "I've been thinking about you all week!"

"Really?"

He didn't speak again for a while, and I thought he'd hung up. But then his voice came back a little stronger. "What have you been up to, anyway? Did you meet any guys you like? I mean, has anyone asked you out yet?"

My voice trembled. "I met a lot of guys. And a lot of girls. But, no, I'm not dating anyone. I really don't want to." Only you, I wanted to add.

"Anna." His voice was strained now. "When I come back—when I can see again—I wonder—" I pressed my ear close to the phone to hear, his voice had faded away again. He was breathing hard, but soon he had gathered up his courage. "I'd like to ask you out. We could go to the movies, or maybe roller-skating, or even to the Halloween Dance. What do you think? Anna, are you there?"

My mouth went dry as I tried to answer. "I'd like that," I whispered into the phone.

Suddenly the living room door opened, and Dad stepped through. "Anna, please don't stay on the phone too long. Someone may be trying to get us for reservations."

"Okay, Dad," I grumbled. "I have to go now," I told Michael. "I guess you'll be so busy looking at things on Monday, you won't have time to call."

"Don't be crazy." He chuckled. It was so good to hear him laugh again. "Calling you will be one of the first things I do. What time do you get home?"

I looked up at my father's impatient face as I quickly answered. "Not until four—the long bus ride. You certainly should know, you rode it long enough."

"Okay, Anna, I'll call you after four, but I don't know how I'll be able to wait so long."

We said goodbye, and I sighed, wishing that our conversation hadn't been cut short.

Dad put his arm around me. "Sorry, honey. But I bet after Michael comes home and you can see him in person, the phone won't seem that important."

I walked up the flight of stairs to my room on the third floor. I stood in front of the bathroom mirror for a long time looking at my brown eyes and my dark hair. "You can see him in person." I repeated my father's words to the girl in the mirror. "But then he'll be able to *see* you, too. What then?"

Chapter Twelve

On Monday afternoon I flew off the bus, dashed into the house, and guarded the phone like a hawk. It rang once, and Helen took the reservation as quickly as she could without sounding too hasty. "There," she said, patting my hand. "It's all yours. And now we'll have a full house for next weekend."

The Chamber of Commerce had told her September would be slow, but just the opposite was true. Dad thought it was because of the leaves turning so early. Anyhow, things around our inn were really hopping, and my family seemed to love it.

I sat on the antique wooden bench beside the phone in the vestibule. For a long time I willed it to ring, but it remained silent. What was taking Michael so long? Grandma called me to dinner and left the kitchen door open so I'd be sure to hear the phone. She patted my hand.

"Eat, young lady. You'll be a sack of bones if you don't!"

I jabbed at the meat loaf and nibbled on a small piece. I certainly didn't want to have a mouthful of food when Michael called! A tiny bite of mashed potatoes with gravy went down easily, so I shot in a few peas and swallowed fast—just in case. But still no call.

After a while I gave up on dinner and dashed back to my seat in the vestibule. Five forty-five and then six. My father walked by, his eyes looking me up and down. "You're still here? Why don't you go up and do your homework or something? We'll let you know when he calls."

"I'm getting worried now," I said miserably. "He promised he'd call as early as he could."

"Maybe they're keeping him busy with tests."

I shook my head, trying to consider that possibility. "Maybe they have him asleep. They probably don't want him to strain his eyes."

He put his hand on my shoulder. "Go on up, Anna."

"Ten more minutes," I begged. "Just let me stay here ten more minutes."

He frowned. "All right. But no more than ten, agreed?"

I nodded and he went back into the living room.

The vestibule felt like a tomb after he left. My father had decorated the entrance with fine old oil paintings, and I walked from one to the other, my finger tracing the heavy lines of paint as I waited for the phone to ring. I stared into the faces in the paintings, studied the trees, considered the clouds, tried to read the artists' signatures. At last I returned to the hard antique bench by the phone. Six forty-five. I had overstayed and gone back on my promise to my dad.

I touched the phone. I would call *him*. Suddenly a shrill ring pierced the air, and my hand shot away from the phone as if I'd been shocked. I grabbed it. "Michael?"

"Anna!" A woman's voice. It was Mrs. Cartwright.

"Yes! Where's Michael? He said he'd call."

"Anna, I'm calling from my hotel room. I've just left Michael. I've been with him since early this morning before they removed the bandages."

"He's resting then?"

"Yes, dear," she said softly. "I'm calling for him, Anna." There was long silence, and my mind raced as I waited for the news. "Anna, they took off the bandages this morning, and well—the doctor said that the operation proved there'd been no optic nerve damage, that all the damage was confined to the retina, but—"

"But what?" I was nearly frantic.

"They really thought he'd be able to see again," she said as if unable to believe her own words.

I couldn't accept what I was hearing. I wanted to slam down the phone and pretend the call hadn't happened. "You mean it didn't work?"

"Well, the doctors don't like to say 'It didn't work,' " Mrs. Cartwright answered carefully. "Dr. Story says that there's a doctor in France who can do wonders with cases like this, but of course it will be awhile before we can get the money together to do something like that." She went on and on about the operation, but I couldn't focus on her words. All I managed to take in was the fact that she and Michael would be coming home in a few days.

"Wait," I said, my voice trembling. "How's Michael? How's he taking it?"

She sighed heavily, and I could hear the weariness in her voice. "Very badly, I'm afraid." In another moment she was crying. "Very badly," she repeated.

I was crying, too. "Oh, Mrs. Cartwright, I'm sorry. I wish there was something I could do."

"You know, Anna, I was in the hospital room when he talked with you the other day. I couldn't help hearing him ask you out. I went back to

106

the hotel that night feeling so good about you and Michael, but when I asked him to call his girlfriend this afternoon he just said, 'I don't have a girlfriend.' "

My heart sank. I swallowed hard. "I'll come see you when you get back," I told her. "And tell Michael he *has* a girlfriend—whether he wants one or not."

September twenty-second. I had written on the calendar that I used as a diary that this was the day Michael would be calling me. Now I squeezed in the line that his mother had called and that the operation had been a failure.

Suddenly my fears of Michael seeing me for the first time seemed trivial and selfish. Now it would be up to me to try to make him happy without his sight. I kept busy during the next few days searching through the school library for books about blindness. I had to learn all I could about the condition—not only for Michael's sake but for mine, too. Michael was going to be blind forever—and I wasn't sure how I was going to handle that.

Chapter Thirteen

Michael came home the next Friday. I knew because every day since the call I'd hopped on my bike after school and ridden to the general store. That day his mother's car was in the driveway, looking dusty and dirty from the long drive up the mountain. The Closed sign was still on the door, and I took that to mean they didn't want to be disturbed. I could understand that. Michael and his mom both had a lot of heartbreaking adjusting to do. I decided to wait until Saturday to try to see him.

The inn was a whirlwind of activity when I got home. Helen and Grandma were cleaning one of the guest rooms, while my father hid clues all over the house for a mystery game. He was always thinking of ways to entertain the guests, and this latest involved solving a mystery. The game lasted all weekend long, and whoever solved it first won a prize. Last week when he had first tried it, the guests had loved it, but it drove Helen wild.

"I found one guest in the cellar!" she complained. "What if someone fell on those dark steps?"

"We're insured," my father answered, going over the new clue list. "Anyhow, that's a darn good place for a clue! I'll have to plant some down there."

Helen just shook her head and went on with her cleaning.

I spent the rest of the day helping Grandma cook and talking to the guests who arrived that night.

Around two o'clock Saturday afternoon I brushed my hair, put on the perfume that Michael liked, and rode over to the store. Several cars were parked outside.

I slipped in quietly as two customers walked out. Mrs. Cartwright was behind the counter making change. She waved me over when she saw me. "I'm glad you're here," she said. "But don't expect too much, Anna."

"What do you mean?"

"Michael's still upset about the operation," she said. "He may not be very good company today."

Then I saw Michael coming from the back

rooms. My heart skipped a beat. Had I expected him to look different? Of course, there wouldn't be any scars or bruises; the surgery was done with a laser, a beam of light. He looked the same as he always had. His dark hair spilled over his forehead, his frame still so tall, his shoulders wide. He was wearing brown cords and a light blue shirt.

Slowly I approached him. He looked up, his head turning slightly, sensing he was not alone.

A few steps later I stood directly in front of him. I reached out and put a hand over one of his. He pulled away sharply. "Anna?"

I'd planned to laugh and try out an awful welcome-home joke that Cass had told me, but instead I just stood there and said, "Hi, Michael. It's me."

He squared his shoulders and said stiffly, "What can I get for you?"

I coughed and cleared my throat, but my voice still came out raspy. "I just wanted to see you, Michael—and welcome you back."

He walked over to a carton of canned tuna that was sitting in one of the aisles. "We've really been busy this morning, so I'm kind of behind in my work." He dragged the box over to one of the shelves and began to stack the cans neatly. "Look, I'm sorry, but it's not a good time for me to talk."

I followed him over to the shelf. "I've been pretty busy, too," I told him. "Last week I stayed late every afternoon helping decorate for the Oktoberfest. Jake and Bobby and a couple of the other guys unloaded a truckful of hay onto the softball field, and we all made little scarecrows and haystacks. There was a whole bunch left over and we ended up putting it into a gigantic pile and jumping into it like little kids. Bobby says we'll make it into a bonfire when the Oktoberfest is over." I was rambling on, trying to get a reaction from Michael, but he just continued stacking cans as if I weren't there at all. "Uh, I know we haven't talked about it yet, but would you like to go with me?"

"I don't think so."

The words stung, but remembering what Mrs. Cartwright had said I forced myself not to feel hurt. Instead I reached down and grabbed a can from the box and put it on the shelf. "It will go much faster with the two of us working."

Michael turned to me, a scowl on his face. "I can handle it myself," he said gruffly.

"I know. But we've always worked together." I smiled. "Even when you weren't speaking to me."

"Not this time, Anna." He turned his back to me.

"But you said you were busy."

"Right. Which means I don't have time to stand around and talk like this." Abruptly he got up and walked toward the counter. "I'll see you around."

"Michael." I followed him again. "I know what you're doing. You're feeling sorry for yourself. And I know you've got every right in the world to do so, but to tell you the truth it's not very becoming."

He turned to me, his face dark with anger. "Since when have you become the big authority?"

"I don't need to be an authority to recognize self-pity when I see it!"

"And I don't need you to tell me what to do!" he retorted.

I winced at the tone of his voice. "Listen," I said, trying another approach, "I've been doing some reading. About blindness. And though I don't really know what you're going through, I've got a better idea now. And I'm getting ideas about how I can help you. What if I come by on Monday with your new assignments?"

"Forget it," he said, staring straight ahead toward the door. "Mom's arranged to get them for me. You don't have to come around here anymore. In fact, I wish you wouldn't."

It was as if he'd thrown a knife at me. "But, Michael, when you called from the hospital you said you wanted to go out with me."

His laugh was bitter. "I must have been loaded with painkillers. Forget it, Anna, I didn't know what I was talking about."

I took a deep breath and blinked furiously, trying not to cry. Whether he was feeling sorry for himself or not, Michael didn't want me around now, and there was nothing I could do about it. I pushed myself away from the counter and started for the door. "So long, Michael," I called, hoping he couldn't hear me crying.

So long, I repeated to myself as I rode home. *And please,* I added, *don't let this be the final goodbye.*

Chapter Fourteen

I didn't visit Michael or the store in the next few weeks. I wanted to give him time to recover from the disappointment of the operation, and truthfully, I wasn't ready to handle more rejection.

Instead, I spent most of my afternoons at Carlyle's, which is the closest thing to a hangout that there is in Blue Mountain. Then there was the Oktoberfest. The entire school showed up for the event, which consisted of a parade, crafts exhibits, games, and tons of food to eat. The best part was the huge bonfire, bright enough to be seen for miles. I stood around it with Cass and Laura and the rest of my new friends, singing songs and feeling giddy in the crisp October night. At the end we all held hands, and in that moment I truly felt I belonged on the mountain.

A few weeks later was the Halloween Dance. Naturally I didn't go with Michael. Cass dragged me along. Neither one of us had a date, and since we were all wearing costumes it was hard to tell who was with whom anyway. Once the music started a few boys asked me to dance, and I fell right into the spirit of the night.

Yet not an hour went by that I wasn't thinking about Michael and how he was coping. Late at night, when I was supposed to be asleep, I read all those books about blindness I'd dragged home from the library. My goal was to learn more about blindness than even Michael knew and maybe figure out a way to help him.

One book was about a woman in Iowa who'd been teaching elementary school for many years. One day a blind girl was assigned to her class, and because she wasn't sure how to work most effectively with her, the teacher began to take special classes. She became so engrossed, she ended up teaching in a school for the blind. I was fascinated with her story and read it in one sitting.

The day I had to take the books back to the school library, I was sitting in the kitchen with my grandmother before the school bus came.

"Grandma, I'm almost sixteen," I began.

She looked up from the apples she was peeling and smiled. "The last time I looked you were twelve. Don't worry, Anna, I won't forget your birthday."

"It's not that I think you'll forget, Grandma," I said, shifting the pile of books on the table. "It's these. I thought I was reading them because of Michael, but now I think I'm doing it because of me."

She wiped her hand on her apron and poked at one of the books. "They're about blind people?"

I nodded my head. "Dad said a long time ago that I would make a good teacher. At first I thought it was a dumb idea, but now I'm beginning to feel interested in a way. Do you think it's too late to change my mind about what I want to be?"

Grandma slowly began to pare the apples she had peeled before answering. Finally she smiled widely at me. "It's never too late! Look at me. Never in my wildest dreams did I think I'd be a cook—but that's what I am, and I'm loving it! Maybe that's what I should have been all along. Look at all the time I wasted sitting around, trying to knit and do stuff I'm really not good at!" She picked up a pie plate and dusted it off with a clean towel. "Now you—you're just beginning. You can go to college and study whatever you want. You may even change your mind after you get there."

"But I was so sure I wanted to design clothes,

Grandma. Remember all the clothes I made for my paper dolls? And that prize I won in ninth grade?"

"I remember," she said. "But this doesn't mean that you can't design clothes or draw as a hobby. Personally, I'm glad you're thinking about teaching instead. You'd make a fine teacher."

"You really think so?"

Grandma smiled. "Why not? You've always loved kids, you're patient, and you're never willing to give up on a person—all good qualities a teacher needs."

I slid off the stool, clutching my books to me. Quickly I placed a kiss on her warm, rosy cheek. "Thanks, Grandma. You're the greatest!" I flew out of her kitchen and headed for the bus.

Later that day Michael stood with his back to me, refusing to admit I was in the store. I knew he could hear my sigh as I leaned on the counter, waiting for him to speak first. The store was empty because it was around dinnertime. I had eaten earlier with Grandma and been excused from the chores so that I could be here.

Grandma was right about me. I was very willing to bide my time, waiting for Michael to come around. But every person has a limit to her patience, and I'd finally reached mine. I refused to give him more time. "Michael, it's me. I haven't come to buy anything. The store is empty, your mother is in the back, and I want to talk to you."

He turned around slowly. "I'm busy now," he said. His face looked strained, his eyes troubled.

"You are *not* busy. I called your mother awhile ago, and she said she'd make sure you wouldn't be."

"What does she have to do with it?"

"Get your jacket," I said, ignoring his question. "We're going for a walk, down to the pond."

He felt the dial on the Braille watch his mother had given him after the operation. "It's almost dark now."

I laughed, not with embarrassment, but a real laugh. I would have never been able to do it before I had studied all of those books. "What does it matter to you? You're blind, Michael. And you know the way down to the pond better than I do."

"Why the pond?" he asked suspiciously.

"It's as good a place as any." I answered. "It's a school night, so I can't stay out late. But if I'm going to go out with you, then we should be *going* someplace together. Agreed?"

He gasped, then his face broke into a crooked smile, the first I'd seen since he'd arrived back from Los Angeles. "You have nerve!"

"And it's about time!" I told him, reaching out

to touch his arm. "Now are you going to go back there and get your jacket—or am I?"

I saw his mother come through the doorway then, smiling. "Hello, Anna, it's been too long." She turned to her son. "Your jacket's exactly where you left it."

It seemed like an eternity before he returned wearing his parka.

Mrs. Cartwright stepped in front of him as he walked toward me. "Michael, this would be a fine time to try using Dr. Story's present."

He shook his head. "I told you what I thought of that 'present'—you can send it back to Dr. Story."

"But you might as well start now," she insisted, going toward the back room. I was puzzled until she returned with a new white cane.

"No," he said angrily, pushing the cane away. "I'm not going to use this thing!"

"It's as good a time as any to start," his mother said firmly.

"I told you—"

"Michael, please," she said, and something in her voice must have changed his mind.

"Okay, okay," he muttered. "I'll take it along, but I don't know what good it'll do!"

Carefully we crossed the road in front of the store and headed down the path toward the pond. The tip of Michael's cane pressed against the hard gravel in the store's parking lot and then on the hard surface of the road. The wind loosened the last leaves on the trees as we carefully made our way on the carpet of leaves covering the ground.

"It was nice of the doctor to send this," I told him as we walked down the hill.

"It came yesterday," Michael said angrily. "I hate it. I must look like an old man," he grumbled.

"Not to me," I told him. "Or to your friends."

"People will notice me."

"So what? Everyone around here knows you. And don't you think you would stand out more without the cane—bumping into things?"

"I suppose," he mumbled.

I saw him swallow hard, his face tense as the cane hit something hard. Haltingly he stepped over a stone. Then he took my arm so he could tell if I stepped down slightly or stopped.

The moon was hidden behind the clouds, making the night very dark, and Michael realized we'd reached the clearing next to the pond before I did. "We're here," he said as he stopped short.

"So we are," I said, but I could barely see the edge of the pond. "Let's sit down." I unfolded the blanket I'd been carrying and spread it out on a flat rock. "It wasn't all that hard, was it?" I asked as I knelt down.

He shrugged. "You were with me."

"You'll do it alone someday. You just needed someone to get you going."

We sat close together, the cold wind whipping around us. "Any skaters out?" he asked.

"Too dark," I answered.

"Right," he said with a chuckle. "I should have remembered."

"Not necessarily," I said. "I mean when it's six o'clock in the summer it's still light out. It's funny how the same time of day can be so different at different times of the year. I always wondered how it would be if you could keep moving the time around so it always stayed light—"

"Anna." I knew I was rambling again and thought he was going to tell me to shut up—or at least change the subject.

"What?"

"Why did you come?"

It was such a simple question, yet I had a hard time getting myself to speak. "I wanted to," I finally managed to say.

"That's hard to believe after our last little 'discussion.' I wasn't exactly polite."

"Horrid is the word for it," I assured him with a grin. "You were pushing me away—and I let you."

"All right," he gave in, "I was horrid. But I

122

didn't want you to see me like this. After the way the operation went, I didn't want you hanging around feeling sorry for me."

"I know. That's why I didn't come back until now. And I did feel sorry for you, Michael. But who wouldn't, knowing the hopes you had for seeing again. I know it's a rough thing to accept, and the last thing I wanted to do was make you think I was here only out of pity. So I stayed home, read some more books about blindness, and took the time to really sort out my feelings about you." I breathed in deeply. "That's why I've got to find out now. Do you still want me to leave?"

"Oh, no." Suddenly Michael reached out and gently brushed my hair back from my face. Tears sprang to my eyes as his fingers traced my cheek.

"What's wrong?" he asked softly.

"Oh, Michael, don't ever hurt me like that again. Don't ever let me think you don't care for me."

"I do," he said quietly. "I have all along. But can you really deal with having a boyfriend who's blind?"

"I don't know," I told him honestly. "I've never even had a boyfriend before. All I know is that blind or not, you're the only one I want to be with. I think about you all the time, and these last weeks—I've missed you terribly."

He took me in his arms and held me close. His hand stroked my hair, silently reassuring me. For a while I let myself forget everything except the sensation of being safe in Michael's arms.

At last he released me. "You know," he said, "I *am* trying to deal with this, but it's hard to accept a verdict of blindness. I feel like I'm giving in, losing hope, and I just can't let that happen. There's this doctor in France. He performs an operation that Dr. Story thinks could fix my eyes. But he might as well be on Mars. I'll never have the money—"

"What about your education fund?"

He shook his head. "My mom says we have to be realistic. I'll need an education now more than ever if I'm going to support myself. Besides, even that's not enough money. I've just got to face it, Anna. I'm blind."

It was the first time I'd ever heard him say those words. Even though they sounded so final, I knew for Michael it was the first and most important step toward rejoining the world.

Chapter Fifteen

A week later, just before Thanksgiving, I got the shock of my life. I got on the school bus and there, in the back, with a sly smile on his face was Michael.

I dropped my books, and nearly fell into Cass's lap. "Michael!" I shrieked.

He grabbed my arm when I drew near and pulled me down into the seat. "Surprised?"

What could I say? I was overwhelmed. He hadn't even hinted at doing something like this.

"I wanted it to be a surprise." He hesitated. "Well, really, I wanted to see if I could do it. If I couldn't, I was prepared to forget the whole thing."

Michael went on to explain that the night before his mother and Mr. Serrano, the school principal, had spent two hours going over the school with him. "First you have to go down the three steps from the bus, then walk fourteen steps on the ground to the cement steps. There are exactly twelve of them before you reach the landing and the front door."

"How can you remember all that?"

He grinned. "I always was good with numbers."

I squeezed his hand in support. "Scared?" I asked.

"Yes," he answered. "But I'll be all right with this." He lifted the cane held tightly in this other hand.

The bus started to fill up with kids, and eventually everyone came over to greet Michael. He laughed and talked about old times with his friends. As we approached the school, though, his smile faded. I knew he was worried about what lay ahead of him.

The bus groaned to a stop. It was time to get off. He bent down and whispered in my ear, "I'll have to borrow your arm for a few days. Okay?"

"Fine," I whispered back. "I'm sure it'll be only a few days."

I walked in front of him and he put his hand on my right shoulder. The other kids tried not to look at us, but they did. I saw admiration in their faces, and I wished that Michael could see it, too. Down the aisle we walked at the same pace as the others. When I reached the steps I climbed down as usual, looking back at Michael. His hand had left my shoulder and he was on his own.

I saw him bite his lip and then carefully step down, his white cane touching the step before he did. Finally he reached the ground without disaster. I sighed with relief and so did everyone watching. There was a hush as Michael and I walked the path side by side, his left hand under my right elbow, his right hand on the white cane. I could hear him count to fourteen under his breath.

As we climbed the twelve cement steps I could hear him counting again, but I don't think anyone else could. It all went so well, I wanted to cry. Cass stood at a distance from us, watching everything. Someone held open the door for him, and I told him that so he wouldn't feel around for the metal handle.

The school was busy and loud as usual, with everyone hurrying to their classes. Michael stepped away from me. "I'm on my own now, Anna. I'll see you at lunch."

"It's a date," I said, hardly believing how natural it felt. "But you'll have to pick *me* up," Michael added with a grin. "Meet me outside room twenty-five—my last morning class. Then we can walk to the cafeteria together. I don't have that down in my head yet."

He touched my arm and let his hand slide down to my hand, squeezing it in his. He bent his head down to meet mine. "Thanks for everything," he said softly.

I left him there, looking back again to see if he was okay. I saw him feel the door frame and then disappear into his homeroom. I looked up and saw Cass waiting for me. "He's going to be okay," I told her.

She laughed, adjusting her books in her arms. "Lucky guy," she said. "He has you. Yeah, he's going to be just fine!"

From that day on Michael attended school like the rest of us, except he kept his tape recorder beside him every minute, recording his classes so he could listen to the lectures when he arrived home. At school he took a few tests by writing the answers on a typewriter accompanied by a reader who would ask each question. A few teachers talked to him about using the Braille system, but he said that would be in the future for him. Right now he would do it all this way.

Michael was doing well in school, but he still cut himself off from his friends. He joked around with Bobby and Les and Cass, but none of us could ever persuade him to come out after school, even to Carlyle's. Michael's world didn't extend beyond school and the store.

I was still reading books on the blind, trying to figure out something that Michael would want to do that would just be fun. It certainly wasn't suggested in any of the books, but somehow I became convinced that ice skating was exactly what he needed. After all, I reasoned, skating was a skill like bicycle riding—once you learned, you never forgot. And, if we could find a time when the pond was clear, he wouldn't have to worry about bumping into anyone.

It was early December before I got up enough nerve to ask Michael to go ice skating with me. I could have predicted his angry outburst.

"Me? I'm lucky if I can walk a straight line with my cane without bumping into a million things! Now you want to put *blades* on my feet?"

"Yes," I answered simply. "What's the matter? Afraid to make a fool out of yourself?"

"Yes." At least he was being honest now.

I finally got him to agree to go late one Saturday afternoon when the light would be fading and all the skaters gone for the day.

We were giggling like two fools when we crossed the road, Michael's white cane tapping along on the hard surface, his skates thrown across his left shoulder, me with a blanket and my skates, carrying a gas lantern Mrs. Cart-wright had insisted we take.

At the pond we put the blanket and lantern down on a rock and laced up our skates. I went out first, testing the ice. It was perfect. The sun was sinking below the horizon, but there was enough light filtering through the bare tree branches to give me a clear vision of the entire surface of the pond. The lantern lit up the grassy area at the edge of the pond.

I turned back to get Michael, but he seemed frozen to the rock. "I don't remember how to skate," he said miserably.

"It's like riding a bike—you can't forget how to skate," I protested. "I'll guide you over to the ice," I promised, taking his arm.

After his first step on the ice, his ankles wig-gled a little, but then he straightened up with the next few steps. I led the way, and he re-laxed. Side by side we skated for a while, laugh-ing and talking and feeling good. Then Michael asked me to take him out to the middle and leave him there so he could try some figure work.

"I'm right over here," I assured him from the edge of the pond. "I'll keep talking to you so you'll know where I am."

He did a few circles on the ice, gradually doing a nice figure eight. He even skated well backward. "Ice hockey," he explained with a smile. A sudden breeze came up, blowing a few brittle leaves onto the ice, and then a branch skimmed the middle of the pond.

"Michael, watch out," I shouted. I was too late. The branch tangled in his blades, and down he went, landing on his backside. Quickly I skated over. "Are you all right?" At first I thought he was in pain, but when he realized I was standing over him he grinned, looking a little bashful.

"I'm okay," he insisted as we left the ice. "No wounds—except maybe my pride." But my knees shook as I guided him back to our blanket. *He could have been hurt*, I thought. I'd have to be more careful when I left him alone.

"You know I heard it," he said, tilting his head to the wind. "I heard the branch sailing across the ice, but I didn't pay attention. I guess I was so carried away. I was trying to pretend it was like it used to be when Lisa and I—"

Suddenly he realized what he was saying. "It's cold out here," he quickly said, clapping his wool gloves together.

I tried to ignore the mention of Lisa, but it seemed to echo through the air.

As if sensing my distress, Michael reached out for my hand. I placed it in his. Then his cold face found mine, his lips brushing across my icy cheeks to my mouth. He kissed me long and tenderly. For a moment I completely forgot Lisa.

"That was nice," he said, his voice husky with emotion.

"Mmmm." I was too happy to think of a coherent answer.

"And you're nice," he went on. "But you're freezing. Come on, we'd better move." With a laugh he stood up, a little wobbly on the skates but with a confidence I hadn't seen in him before. He held his hands out to me.

"Michael."

"What?"

"I don't want to go back yet."

He put an arm around my shoulder and drew me to his side. "I didn't say anything about going back, did I?"

"No, but—"

"Don't you want to skate with me?" he asked. "We've got to do *something* to stay warm out here."

I hugged him so hard I thought we were both going to fall over. Then, carefully, we made our way back onto the ice.

This time we skated together, holding hands, playing at skating apart and then drawing close again. We moved slowly as if there were something very fragile between us. For a while we didn't talk at all, just concentrated on the delicious sensation of gliding across the ice.

It was Michael who broke the silence. "Only you," he said.

"Only me what?"

"Only you could have gotten me to do this."

"I needed a skating partner," I said, trying to sound casual.

He stopped skating and pulled me toward him. "I needed a lot more than that," he said. "I needed a friend like you, and I didn't even know it."

Suddenly I felt nervous. Michael was getting serious—about a girl whom he thought looked exactly like Lisa.

"Michael, what do you want to be?" I said, changing the topic as quickly as I could.

"A professional hockey player," he replied sarcastically. He shook his head, as if he couldn't figure out what was wrong with me.

We carefully made a big swirling turn at the end of the pond. "What about you?" he asked, obviously trying to humor me. "Oh, I remember. You told me you wanted to be a fashion designer."

"Not anymore," I said. "I've been thinking I'd like to be a teacher."

"And spend all day caring for little brats?" he asked teasingly.

"Little *blind* brats, as a matter of fact." I stopped in the middle of the pond. "I want to work with blind children." I held my breath, waiting for it to sink in. "What do you think?"

He encircled me in his arms. He drew his fingers through my hair, and twisted one finger around a few strands, making a curl. Drawing me to him, he bent his head and laid his cheek against mine. "Anna," he said into my ear, "I think I've fallen in love with you."

Later, long after I'd walked back to the store with Michael and then bicycled home, I lay awake in bed. The full moon shone through the window, casting a white light across my comforter, reminding me of what it felt like to be skating under that moon with Michael. And what it had felt like to hear him say he had fallen in love with me.

Those were the words I'd wanted to hear more than any others, and yet it didn't feel right. I just couldn't help wondering if Michael really loved me, or was in love with some imaginary girl who looked just like Lisa. A substitute. I knew that soon I would have to tell him the truth. I needed to know that I was the one he was in love with and not Lisa's shadow.

In the meantime, while I gathered my courage, I'd ask Cass if she had an old yearbook, one that Lisa was in. Maybe I was asking for trouble, but I wanted to actually *see* my competition.

Helen would have called me crazy. She would have said, "Lisa is dead, Anna." But Helen would have been wrong. Lisa was still very much alive— inside Michael's dreams.

Chapter Sixteen

Cass thought I was absolutely nuts when I asked her if she had any pictures of Lisa that I could see, but she agreed to show me what she could. She'd bought the school's yearbook in her freshman and sophomore years and brought them over to the inn a few days later.

She threw the yearbooks on the middle of my bed. "Why are we doing this?" she asked. "I mean, why can't you just be happy Michael likes you—and let it go at that?"

I couldn't answer her. It was crazy, but I just had to know what Lisa looked like. I shook my head. "Come on, Cass, my grandmother will be calling us down to dinner in half an hour. Let's just do it."

We propped ourselves up on the pillows and

went through the first book. "That's when she was a sophomore," Cass said, pointing at a photo of the drama club. "There she is in the second row. She starred in *Carousel* that year. She was so scared every performance, she actually shook all during the first two scenes, but then when it came her turn, she just ran out there and she was wonderful!"

I stared at the beautiful, fine-boned face. Lisa was smiling, looking as if she were about to break into laughter. But it was her eyes that made her look as if she were lit up inside with mischief or— I realized what it was—of all the kids in the picture Lisa was the one who looked most alive.

Cass flipped over the pages. "Here she is on the staff of the newspaper. She's the one holding up one of the issues with the senior editor."

It seemed to me the senior editor was more interested in Lisa than he was in the paper. He clearly had one arm around her. Michael was in that shot, too, but in the last row, peering over the heads of the others. I was sure they put him back there because of his height.

Cass turned quickly to other shots with Lisa in them. A Ping-Pong tournament showed her laughing, reaching out with her paddle. It looked as though she had hit the ball. Of course, she wouldn't miss it. She was one of the finalists.

In the yearbook that showed her as a junior, she was into even more things. There she was in a racing suit, posing to make a dive into the pool, her long hair pushed into one of those awful regulation caps. Still, she looked great.

I peered at the girls' basketball team. "Well, at least she isn't in this one," I said smugly. "Too short."

"But you'll notice she made the baseball team," Cass said, laughing. "See? Here she is making a home run."

There were more pictures, lots of casual photos of Michael and Lisa together. Usually they were holding hands, or Michael's arm was around her tiny waist.

I moaned. "What a lousy thing to do to myself! Honest, Cass, why didn't you just say you didn't have anything to show me!"

She giggled and closed the last one with a bang. "You asked for it, dummy!"

I threw a pillow at her, and she picked it up and threw it right back. "Now, listen, Anna, my stupid friend! I like you for who you are. Why do you think Michael doesn't?"

I picked up the pillow she'd thrown and hugged it to my chest. "It's just that Michael has never seen me—"

"And never will," she said softly, a frown puckering her brow.

"I guess you're right," I agreed. "Even if he could get to France, he'd never be able to afford that operation. The surgeon is so famous." I sighed and rested my head on the headboard. "You'd think there would have been some insurance or something from the accident."

Cass got up off the bed and stretched, her long arms reaching for the ceiling. "No. I remember reading about it in the newspaper. The drunk driver paid his bail, then left the state. No one ever found him. Jake had just gotten his driver's license a couple of days before and his parents hadn't put him on the policy, so their insurance company wouldn't pay. As it was they barely had enough money to pay for the hospital bills."

I nodded. "It must have been awful. All those families hit like that."

Cass went over to the back window to watch the snow. It was really coming down now. "It was." She sighed. "The town helped out some. The PTA had some bake sales, and Michael's class washed cars to raise money. I don't think they made a lot, but I suppose it was some help."

That gave me an idea. Maybe I could come up

with another fund-raising plan so Michael could go to France for that special operation. I decided I'd talk to him first, to see what he thought of the idea. But as it turned out, I didn't have to. . . .

Chapter Seventeen

Michael called me one afternoon just before Christmas vacation.

"What's up?" I asked. "I just saw you ten minutes ago."

He seemed out of breath, and his words just tumbled out. "Anna, listen, you won't believe it. Dr. Story sent me a letter. He wants me to go to Boston!"

I didn't understand. "Why Boston?"

"Because that doctor—you know the one in France? Well, he's going to be spending some time at a Boston hospital. Dr. Story wrote to him—anyhow, this French doctor, Dr. Boulez, thinks he can help me. He uses something called the Argon Laser Surgical Procedure that can repair damage to the retina."

I was so speechless, all I could do was scream.

Michael started to laugh, sounding almost hysterical. "Here's the best part. He wants to do it as a demonstration—to show the students. That means he'll do it for nothing!"

I slid right off the antique bench in the vestibule. "For nothing?"

He couldn't stop laughing. "All we have to do is pay for the trip there and back. They're going to pay for a hotel room for my mother, and I'll be spending the time at the hospital."

"When? How soon?" My jaw was trembling so hard I could hardly get out the words.

"January fifth."

I could hear Mrs. Cartwright in the background. "We'll leave here the weekend before," she told him excitedly.

"Listen, can you come over? I want to talk to you."

I bit my lip to stop the trembling. "I'll be right there!"

I raced past Helen in the kitchen, shouting the news to her. She dropped a dish towel, and her mouth flew open. Then I dashed into the living room, grabbed my father's hand as he was picking up the newspaper, and shouted to him that Michael was going to Boston as I headed for the front door.

I still had on my jacket and boots, so there was nothing to hold me up. Down the road I ran, slipping on patches of ice, but I guess I was running too fast to fall. I was practically airborne.

Bursting into the warmth given off by the old Franklin stove, I grabbed Mrs. Cartwright and swung her around until we both were dizzy. She kissed me soundly on the cheek. "Did you ever hear of such a Christmas present?" she asked, laughing.

Michael came in from the back of the store. "Boy, did you fly! I practically just put the phone down!"

Mrs. Cartwright insisted I stay for dinner, which worked out just fine. I don't think I could have left if I'd tried.

Dinner was giddy and wonderful. Mrs. Cartwright explained that the hospital in Boston was huge and very prestigious. Michael tried to con her into taking a side trip to Florida, since they were finally going to the East Coast. Then we all began talking about the places we'd never been to but dreamed of visiting, and before I knew it, dinner was over. Mrs. Cartwright got up to clear the table.

"Let me help you," I said.

"No, that's all right," she said. "You stay with Michael. Just do me one favor. Talk him out of Florida."

I watched Michael's face as his mother left the room. With a pang, I realized it was filled with the same hope I'd seen before the last operation. I didn't know what to say. Since the night on the pond when he had told me he loved me, I'd been careful around Michael, trying to stop myself from falling even more hopelessly in love than I already was. Sooner or later he'd discover my lie, and I couldn't bear to think about what would happen then.

"So, who's your date for the New Year's Eve party?" he asked, smiling. Kelly Bruce was throwing a big party at her house, and all of Blue Mountain was going to be there.

"I hadn't thought that far ahead," I said honestly.

"Well, start thinking," he said with a grin. "Because I've been thinking—no matter what happens with this operation, it's time I returned to the land of the living."

"You mean you really want to take me?" I couldn't believe what I was hearing.

He frowned. "Isn't that what I just said?"

"Yes, but—"

"Anna," he said, cutting me off, "would you please give me a straight answer? Will you be my date on New Year's Eve?"

"Yes," I cried. "Yes, yes, yes, yes!"

He laughed as I hugged him. "That's what I figured."

Once we'd gotten the New Year's question settled, we went on to discuss the upcoming Christmas vacation, and Les's latest plans to take Michael tobogganing. Michael insisted Les was a kamikaze at heart and swore the only way he'd agree to go was if *he* was steering the toboggan.

Neither of us mentioned the operation again until Michael walked me to the door. His face seemed suddenly serious as he bent to kiss me on the forehead. "Anna, what if this operation doesn't work?" he asked quietly. "I mean there's no guarantee. Just like the last time."

I threw my arms around him and held him close. "Then, Michael, at least you'll know you gave it your best shot."

He gave me a rueful smile. "That's what my mom says. You know," he went on, "this has been the strangest winter."

"What do you mean?"

"When I came back after the first operation, I gave up. I swore I'd never leave the store again. It was like every dream I'd ever had had died."

"And now?" I asked.

"I feel like a little kid again," he said softly. "Anything seems possible—going back to school, skating, asking you out—" His voice trembled. "Maybe even having my sight back. All of a sudden I can dream about the future again."

For a moment I thought about what Michael

had said. He was right—these past few months had been strange and very different from what I'd expected. All my dreams—of going back to Rutherford and becoming a fashion designer—had been replaced. I had new hopes for the future, shimmering new winter dreams of Michael being able to see again and still loving me afterward.

I was picturing the two of us together when he bent his head and kissed me good night. *Sometimes*, I thought, *reality can be as sweet as a dream.*

The day before Christmas I went ice skating with Michael on our pond. There were a few other kids when we got there, but they soon left. Most people had little time for skating on Christmas Eve; there were still packages to be wrapped, last-minute things to do, friends to visit and wish a merry Christmas. Michael and I had finished all our shopping and decided to skate for about an hour in the late afternoon.

As we waited for the other skaters to leave the ice, we sat talking on our rock.

"You know," Michael told me, "lately, I can feel a person's mood by shaking his or her hand. Isn't that weird? Like when Mrs. Morgan came into the store last night. Her fingers were sort of stiff and trembling, so I knew she was upset. Then today I found out that her husband had just lost his job."

"So it really happens," I said.

"What does?" He ran a hand through my hair.

"What those books said. That as a person adjusts to blindness, the other four senses become much sharper."

Michael laughed. "Then you'd better watch out. I know more about you than you think."

I quickly changed the subject. "Tell me about the weather."

He smiled. "Do you mean, how I can tell what it's like outside?"

"Yes," I answered.

"Well, it was sunny," he said. "I can still feel a little warmth even though the sun's going down." He hugged his knees to him. "You know, the most amazing thing is that I can identify a tree by the way the wind whips through it. In the wind the leaves of a maple have a deeper, fuller sound than the needles of a pine tree."

"I've never noticed," I told him, impressed.

"I never really heard the cars drive up to the store before the way I do now," he said, putting on his skates. "And the school bus has a certain smell." He turned to me. "Are you wearing anything around your neck, today? Yesterday it was that necklace of shells. I recognized the sound they make."

I felt around my neck. Underneath my heavy scarf was a gold chain. "The links are so tiny," he said softly. "Is there anyone around now?"

I surveyed the empty pond and woods. "No. They're all gone at last."

He bent and kissed me. "Soon I'm going to be able to see you, Anna. Not just hold you, but really *see* you."

That was the problem, I told myself miserably as I stiffened under his caress.

Chapter Eighteen

On Christmas morning, before I went down to join my family and open the presents, I wrote on my calendar: "The most beautiful day I've ever seen." Just a few hours away, down in Rutherford, I knew the palm trees were swaying, and the temperatures were in the seventies. That was the Christmas weather I was used to. Now, for the first time, I looked out my window at a Christmas morning that looked like a traditional holiday scene.

I could see sparkling white snow covering all the hills, and I knew it was cold enough out there to see my own breath in the air. Nothing could be as lovely as Blue Mountain that day, I thought. I had to laugh. I hadn't wanted to come here, and now I never wanted to leave. I was always so reluctant to make changes, and

Helen said that wasn't a very good way to be. Life, she said, was one change after another.

As it turned out, I was the last one downstairs. Dad and Helen had decided to close the inn for the holidays, and I was glad we didn't have to share our celebration with strangers. I didn't have to wonder what I was getting from Dad and Helen. Spread out under the huge tree in the living room was my very own set of skis. And wrapped up in a brightly colored box was a complete skiing outfit.

"I can't wait to show Cass," I said. "She's been begging me to go skiing with her."

My father was opening his present from me, a huge gold-rimmed log book. "Just what I wanted!" he said. "Helen, look at this! Now I can throw away that old guest book I've been using." He smiled at me. "Thanks, kitten."

Helen held up the brown silk blouse I'd given her. "It's gorgeous," she announced. "I love it, Anna!"

Grandma handed me a package from under the tree. She had tied three bells on the ribbon and it jingled pleasantly as I reached for it. I knew it was something she'd made. It was kind of a joke in our family—Grandma loved to knit even though she was really terrible at it, and as a result we all had some pretty strange clothing.

She sat back on the rocking chair. "I only hope it fits!"

Quickly I removed a beige sweater from the tissue paper and held it up to myself. "Oh, it'll fit, Grandma," I assured her. "They're wearing them really baggy this year."

She frowned as she examined the sweater more closely. "I don't know, Anna. The right arm seems to be longer than the left, and somehow the back never got as long as the front."

"Never mind," I said, laughing. "I love it!" With a flourish I whipped out her present. "Here, Grandma, wear it in good health."

Tearing open the package, she "oohed" and "aahed" at her new rose bathrobe. Still, I had a sneaky feeling she would just put it away in a drawer and continue to wear her trusty old chenille one that was barely holding together at the seams.

We spent the rest of the morning opening more presents and eating a huge breakfast of sausage, eggs, biscuits, and fruitcake.

It was close to noon before I left for Michael's house. The first thing I saw when I entered the store was a tall, fragrant Christmas tree set up on the rug. "Like it?" Michael asked after greeting me with a kiss. "I put it up myself."

"It's beautiful," I said, feeling very proud of him.

Michael and I sat down next to it, the rich smell of his mother's coffee perking in the air. "I brought something for you," I said as I put a box in his hands.

I watched him wrestle briefly with the wrapping paper. I had spent weeks knitting Michael a scarf that he could wear ice skating. It was the first thing I'd ever knitted for anyone, and to my surprise, the results weren't half-bad. Even Grandma had been impressed.

"It's royal blue with flecks of yellow and red," I said as Michael lifted the scarf from the box and draped it around his neck. "It matches your coat."

"Thanks, Anna," he said softly. "It will always remind me of you—and the time we spent together on the pond."

With shaking hands I opened his present to me. At first I thought it was a small photo album because of the size of the box. The tan leather-bound book felt smooth in my hand as I pulled it out of the tissue paper. "A diary," I said, opening the gold clasp. "How'd you know I've always wanted one? I scribble all over my calendar."

"Cass told me," he said, laughing. "I asked her for ideas, and the first thing she thought of was your calendar. Do you like it?"

I turned it over in my hands. "I love it, Michael. I just wish I didn't have to wait until the new year to write in it."

He flipped it open. "You don't. It's not dated, so you can write in it whenever you want."

That sounded good to me. Some days I love to jot down everything that's happened so I can remember it all, and sometimes I don't feel like writing at all.

Helen had invited Mrs. Cartwright and Michael to the inn for Christmas dinner, so before leaving we made sure all the doors were locked and the damper put on the stove. Michael stepped out on the front stoop before we closed the door. "I can smell the day is great," he said breathing in the good, cold air. "And I can hear my stomach groaning. Let's go!" He put out his white cane, and we started for my house.

Chapter Nineteen

Although it was a Sunday, I woke up early on the morning of January third. This was the day that Michael and his mother would fly to Boston. The next day he'd enter the hospital, and on Tuesday, the fifth, he was scheduled for the operation.

I went down to the kitchen, grabbed some orange juice, and told my grandmother that I was going out for a walk.

Her eyebrows rose behind her glasses. "This early? Oh, you're going to say goodbye to Michael, aren't you?"

"I did that last night," I explained, feeling my throat tighten. "They're probably gone by now."

"He's a nice boy," she said softly. "I hope things work out for him."

I kissed her cheek. "Thanks, Grandma."

I shoved my mittened hands into my jacket pockets, and my feet automatically followed the path down to the pond. The snow started to fall again, bringing an eerie silence to the woods. It fell so softly, effortlessly. It had always amazed me that such soft flakes could actually pile up into huge, solid drifts.

I sat down near the pond on our favorite stone, the one where we'd always spread out the blanket. That day I had no blanket for comfort, but I sat there anyway, looking out over the empty pond. With the snowfall everyone had abandoned skating for skiing.

There was a lot I needed to think about. The last two days had gone by in a whirl. First there'd been New Year's Eve. Michael and I had gone out for dinner with Cass and Bobby, who she'd decided "wasn't so bad, after all." Then we'd all gone to Kelly's party. And though Michael was calm, I was terrified. I don't know what I was afraid of—both of us stumbling into the punch bowl or some other disaster. But none of my nightmares materialized. Most of what I remember were Michael's friends crowding around him, glad to have him back, and then Michael pulling me aside just before the clock struck midnight, so that when the new year came in I was in his arms for a kiss that left me breathless.

If the party worked out better than I expected, the day before hadn't worked out at all. I'd spent the day with Michael and Mrs. Cartwright, helping them mind the store, pack, and finally go to the other side of the mountain to shop for last-minute things.

It was almost nine o'clock when Mrs. Cartwright stopped at the inn to drop me off. Michael and I hadn't had a moment to ourselves.

"Can you wait a minute, Mom?" Michael asked. "I want to walk Anna to the door."

I knew his mom could see us from the car, so our goodbye kiss was quick. I didn't allow myself to cry.

"Be good," he told me, touching my cheek. "I'll miss you."

"You, too." I held him close for just a moment, and then he turned toward the car, his white cane feeling the way before him.

I'd never gotten the chance to tell him any of the things I'd planned to say. *Maybe it was better this way,* I thought as I stared at the empty pond. I closed my eyes and listened to the wind whipping through the pines. I opened my eyes to see a single bird on a snow-laden bush, shaking the white powder from his wings as he chirped softly.

Michael had told me he wouldn't call from Boston unless the operation was a success. I could understand that. It would be too painful to discuss otherwise. I'd have to wait now and be patient.

I closed my eyes again and let the sun warm my face. Suddenly I heard a twig breaking behind me. I turned and saw Michael making his way along the path with his cane.

"Michael! I thought you left!"

He shook his head, and I could see his breath in the cold air. He wore a red snowcap and a heavy brown jacket over winter cords.

"I came to say goodbye again. We stopped at the inn, but your grandmother said you'd gone for a walk."

"How did you know I was here?"

He laughed. "Where else would you have gone?"

His answer forced me to smile, but I didn't feel happy. I hated goodbyes, and now I would have to go through it all over again. But I was glad to see him, if that made sense. Just to have one more moment with him was wonderful.

I put out my hand and pulled him down beside me on the stone. "Michael, I have to tell you something. Something terribly important that I should have told you a long time ago."

He frowned and pushed the red knit cap farther back on his head. "Sounds awful!" He hesitated then asked quietly, "Is there someone else?"

I couldn't tell if he was kidding or not. "Of course not, dummy!" I grabbed his hand and took a deep breath. "Listen, Michael. Remember I told you I had blond hair and blue eyes?" I didn't wait for him to answer. "I don't. My hair is brown—just plain old brown. And my eyes are nothing anyone would look at twice, either. They're just plain, regular-size brown eyes."

I was out of breath from my long-winded confession, but I kept right on going. "My ears are way too big, and I've got lots of freckles—not too many on my face, but loads on my back and arms. What I'm trying to say, Michael, is that I'm not—I'm not—"

"You're not Lisa. I know," he said, reaching out to me. "I've always known that."

I looked into his face. "You have?"

He nodded. "And I don't want you to be anyone but Anna."

He held me tightly in his arms. "The day after the storm I asked my mom to describe you. You know what she did? She led me over to the burlap bag of chestnuts. She pushed my hands down into them and asked me to pick one up. 'Remember how brown these are? Anna's hair is that color.' And then she put my fingers on her ring. She said, 'Remember the emerald your father gave me before he died? Anna's eyes are a deep brown with tiny flecks of this emerald.' And that's how I knew what you looked like."

For a moment I couldn't speak. I couldn't believe he had known all along.

"Anna?" he said. "Are you all right?"

I felt tears welling up in my eyes.

"Anna?"

"I—I just don't want you to hate me for lying," I sniffed.

"Hate you? I could never hate you!"

"And"—the tears were coming uncontrollably now—"I don't want you to be disappointed when you see me."

He held me close, not minding that I was completely soaking the front of his jacket. He waited until I'd calmed down a little, then said, "Anna, I promise you, no matter how it all comes out I won't be disappointed."

Together we walked up to his mother's car. We kissed goodbye, then I watched him ride down the hill headed for the airport and the operation that, one way or the other, would affect him for the rest of his life.

Our next guests arrived, and I threw myself into everything that had to be done. I helped Grandma in the kitchen, did a million things for Helen, helped my father organize a cross-country ski tour, and, in the spare moments, straightened up my cluttered room. Faithfully I wrote in my diary, counting off the days until

Michael would call. Each time I finished a page, I would turn to the next empty one, wondering if that would be the page where I would enter the good news about Michael.

But as the days went by I began to fear the worst. Michael didn't call. I knew they had operated on Tuesday. As in the first operation it would probably be a week or so before they removed the bandages. So I tried not to be too concerned until the following week, concentrating instead on after-school visits to Carlyle's, Cass's growing crush on Bobby, and the never-ending activity at the inn. Cass had begun to teach me how to ski, and we both felt a supreme sense of accomplishment when I finally made it down the beginners' slope without falling.

School went on the same, except the work got harder. Cass and I sat in the bus every morning grumbling about the homework we had to do.

"It's like each teacher doesn't know what the other one gave us to do! Don't they check with one another? How many hours in the day do they think we have!" She threw her long braid over her shoulder. "Honestly, Anna, sometimes I think I won't make it!"

"You're hardly flunking," I told her.

"You haven't seen my last French test." She pulled it out of her bag. "See?"

There was a big D at the top of the page.

"Maybe you ought to start hanging out at Snow Summit. I hear they're hosting a bunch of skiers from the French Alps." I turned back to my own worries. "I wonder if Michael will call today."

Cass shook her head. "You're beginning to sound like a broken record." Then her voice softened. "I'm sure he's got a good reason for not calling."

It had been two weeks. Too long, I thought, for any hope. I wanted to call Boston, but I didn't have the nerve.

In the following days I would rush from the bus, tear into the inn, and find either my father or Helen. Each afternoon they would shake their heads no, and then I'd go upstairs to my room and try not to cry. Finally, I knew it was time to face the facts. The operation hadn't worked—or Michael would have called.

It was the twenty-third day of January, a Saturday, eighteen days after Michael's operation. I spent the morning helping Helen and my father get the guests settled. Then I joined my grandmother in the kitchen for another one of her cooking lessons. That day she was teaching me how to roll out dough for a pie crust. I'd attempted it before, but had never had too much luck. Baking was never high on my list of priorities.

"It's the light touch," she said as she handed me the rolling pin.

Somehow I managed to make a crust without holes in it and successfully got it into the baking pan without tearing it to pieces. Grandma looked as thrilled as if I'd climbed Mount Everest. Maybe she'd make a cook out of me yet.

Then the phone rang. I felt a tug at my heart as if this was the call I'd been waiting for. I held my breath as Grandma reached for the receiver.

The call was for me, but it wasn't the call I wanted. It was Eileen Bliss, asking me to go ice skating with her and her twin sister, Caryn.

I hadn't been to the pond since the day I said goodbye to Michael, and since nothing else was going on I agreed to meet them there. We skated for about two hours. The twins were so good it was disgusting, I thought, as I watched them do a series of fancy spins and axels. But it felt good to be at the pond again—so good that I decided to stick around after the twins chose to call it a day.

I yelled goodbye to them and then realized with a start that the pond was empty. I smiled to myself. Now I could try *my* fancy moves without anyone around to laugh!

I was an adequate skater but never very daring, always sure I'd fall and be laughed off the ice. But with no one there I was free to do

165

whatever I wanted. So in my mind I imagined music, beautiful music like in the *Nutcracker*. For the first time in my life I felt graceful on the ice as I sailed across it like a prima ballerina.

The wind was picking up, and I could feel my cheeks and nose begin to tingle in the frigid air. I knew from experience they had to be bright pink at this point, but I didn't particularly care how I looked.

A few minutes later I heard the sound of applause. For an instant I'd thought I was really dancing on a stage and had come to the end of my performance. Then I snapped to attention and opened my eyes. Someone had seen me. I was too far from shore to tell who it was. Automatically I raised my mittens to my cold face as I skated to the edge.

Halfway there I recognized him. "Michael!" I shouted.

He stood there as tall and beautiful as I remembered him. And there was no white cane.

"You're back," I said, my voice trembling.

Slowly he walked toward me, and, I swear, for a second my heart stopped beating. "You know," he said, "you're not half as bad a skater as you think."

My voice cracked. "You—you saw me! Michael—"

He nodded, smiling. "And what a sight!"

On the tips of my blades I ran to him, and he

caught me in his arms. "Oh, Michael, I'm so happy! But why didn't you call? I was so worried."

"We wanted to make sure it was permanent. There were a lot of tests—"

Before he could finish I tilted my face up toward his and kissed him. Then Michael gently pushed me away and held me at arm's length. "Let me get a good look at you. Oh, Anna, I don't know what you could have been worried about. You're beautiful!"

I covered my face with my mittens again. "Even with my red nose?"

He laughed. "It's the prettiest red nose I've seen all day. Come on. I know someone who makes a mean cup of hot chocolate. Let's get you defrosted."

As I grabbed Michael's hand and we began to wind our way up the hill to the main road, I glanced up at the pine trees fringed with snow. My winter dreams, I thought, had come true after all.

You're going to love
ON OUR OWN®

Starring in a SWEET DREAMS mini-series— Jill and Toni from *Ten Boy Summer* and *The Great Boy Chase*

Is there life after high school? Best friends Jill and Toni are about to find out—on their own.

Jill goes away to school and Toni stays home, but both soon learn that college isn't all fun and games. In their new adventures both must learn to handle new feelings about love and romance.

ON OUR OWN—The books that begin where SWEET DREAMS leaves off.